Pictures
of
Houses
with
Water Damage

stories

Michael
Hemmingson

Black Lawrence Press

Black Lawrence Press
www.blacklawrence.com

Executive Editor: Diane Goettel
Book Design: Steven Seighman

Black Lawrence Press
115 Center Avenue
Pittsburgh, PA 15215
U.S.A.

Published 2010 by Black Lawrence Press, an imprint of Dzanc Books

First edition November, 2010
ISBN-13: 978-0982520420
Printed in the United States

This book is a work of fiction. Real places and events have been changed and fictionalized. All characters are products of the author's imagination and any resemblance to actual persons, living or dead, is entirely coincidental.

Pictures of Houses with Water Damage

Contents

For *you*

and

in memoriam
Barry Hannah
1942 – 2010

Why Don't You Use Your Parking Space?

Mid-afternoon that Saturday I notice my upstairs neighbors have been using my parking space to have a yard sale, although there is no yard attached to this apartment building. They are selling things, everyday things, the things people discard, and they are making some money.

Two women in their late twenties live upstairs, right above my apartment. I often hear their feet as they walk around. One of them is a new tenant; she moved in after the other woman's boyfriend, a rap singer of some sort, moved out.

I'm annoyed. This is my parking space; they are using my space and didn't ask if I needed it, if it was okay.

This bothers me.

I wonder how long they've been at it. I've only noticed it now, mid-afternoon, because I slept until 11:30.

I have a hangover.

I go outside. Only one of the women is there, the new neighbor, she is blonde. She wears big blue-rimmed sunglasses and blue shorts and her blonde hair is in a long ponytail held back by a blue ribbon. I look around at the stuff: clothes, utensils, books, men's shirts, some recording equipment, a turntable, some vinyl records that probably have warped out here under the sun. I wonder if the other woman's ex-boyfriend knows she is selling his rap gear.

The other woman, the neighbor who has been upstairs for two years, is Asian. I don't know what kind of Asian. I know her name is Lisa because when she fought with her ex-boyfriend, he'd yell her name a lot. Lisa this and Lisa that and Lisa you bitch and Lisa *Lisa Lisa stop stop stop it now!*

I approach the blonde woman.

Hi, she goes.

Did you think of asking my permission? I say.

I don't understand, she says.

This is my parking space. I pay rent on it.

Oh, she says; the landlord told Lisa it was okay.

But did you think of clearing it with me?

She goes, All I know is the landlord told Lisa it was okay.

I call the landlord. He did tell her she could use the parking space. But as long as it was okay with you, he says; she was supposed to clear it with you. Are you saying she didn't?

No, she did not.

Young people today, he says. No one asks anymore, no one says 'please' or 'thank you' or 'excuse me' anymore. Have you noticed that? he says.

I think I have, I say.

It's their parents' fault, the landlord says; folks don't teach their kids manners anymore because they don't have manners themselves. Has this inconvenienced you at all?

No, but it could have.

I understand, he says.

If I needed the space . . .

I know; she should have asked.

An emergency . . .

I'll talk to her, he says.

No need . . .

I'll talk to her, he says.

Outside, the blonde girl is saying something to Lisa, who has come down from upstairs. I look out the window. The blonde points at my door. Lisa glares at my door. Her cell phone rings. Her cell phone is in the front pocket of her jeans. She answers it. I know it is the landlord, because when she gets off the phone, the two start to pack things up and take the items back upstairs.

I want to tell her she can stay; she can keep selling. I don't. I expect her to knock on my door and go, Sorry. Or something. She doesn't.

I find the blonde attractive. She looks like someone I was once going to marry and have children with, and then it fell apart and left a hole in my heart, left a fear of getting close to someone again. She looks too much like this woman, this blonde, as I watch her go up and down the stairs.

I'm not sure if it is my imagination or if this is true.

***

For the past month, I have been working on a screenplay set in a science station at the South Pole, titled *It's Very Cold Down Here*. I've been writing it for a producer who will probably not produce it because I've written something for him before and he didn't get the money together, but he did pay me. I have cashed his recent check and I have two more months to get him a ninety-to-one-hundred page script.

It is not coming along well.

I sit at my desk and stare out the window a lot, then type in a scene with a penguin. The window at my desk looks onto my parking space and the courtyard of the building. The past two weeks, I have been seeing the blonde a lot, coming and going, sometimes with a bicycle. Over the course of two weeks, the blonde looks like she is losing weight, perhaps from bike riding or maybe she's not eating like she used to, she goes from slightly chubby to slender and every day she looks more and more like the person I once loved and still love.

Speaking of which, I think it is she, the one I once loved, who has been calling on the phone; it rings now and then, at any hour, and there is no voice on the other line, just breathing. The caller ID is blocked. I am almost certain it is she. Why doesn't she speak? What does she want to say? Why doesn't she just simply say *hi*?

***

After a few weeks I find myself wanting to say hello to the blonde whose name is Heidi because I have heard Lisa and someone else call her Heidi. She looks like a Heidi; sometimes she wears her hair in two braids. It no longer bothers me that she looks like the person I used to love and that I think keeps calling at all hours and not saying a word.

I hear Lisa's new boyfriend, this tall guy with a lot of tattoos whose name I do not know, say something about Heidi's birthday next week. He asks: What are you going to do on your birthday, Heidi?

I don't know, she goes, probably nothing, she says.

You have to do *some*thing, he goes.

I have nothing to do, she goes.

She has nobody, I thought. She's like me; she is alone.

Maybe we'll take you out to dinner, Lisa goes.

You don't have to, Heidi says.

We'd be glad to, Lisa's tall boyfriend with tattoos says.

Oh, don't worry, Heidi goes.

No one should be alone on a birthday, he goes.

I have—before, she goes.

Like me, I think. I remember a birthday, a Thanksgiving, a Christmas, two Christmases, before the one I once loved moved in with me, and we were "dating" (if that was what it was, we were having sex), did not come to see me, be with me. She said society put too much pressure on these days, these events; too much expectation, she said, too much opportunity to disappoint and hurt. She said: Why become a slave to false constructs of celebration? When I showed up at her door with flowers, champagne, and a present, she burst into tears and said: Being kind and romantic is not always the best thing. She said: I'm not used to men being nice to me.

I think about this and I think that Heidi might be the same. She is saying she does not want to celebrate, but deep down she wants attention and gifts and kindness and maybe even some affection.

We'll do something, Lisa says.

If you insist, Heidi says.

We insist, the tall boyfriend with tattoos says.

***

What I do is something stupid but I do it anyway because I think she needs it and it makes me feel good to do it. It also makes me feel devious. And stupid; desperate. I have a vase full of flowers, fifty dollars worth, delivered to her door upstairs. I almost order the flowers from the Internet, but realize I will have to use my credit card, and she could call the company and ask who sent them, because they are going to come from 'A Secret Admirer' and I don't want her to know it is I. Frankly, I have no desire to get to know her, to talk to her, to date her, to be intimate. She looks too much like You Know Who, as I said, and right now I don't need the complication of someone in my life, I have to finish this damn screenplay and make money otherwise I will have to step outside into the world and get a regular job which I hate doing. I'd much rather write screenplays and watch TV and DVDs.

I walk three blocks down the street to a florist that is across the street from a gas station. I pick out some flowers, a blue vase, and write down the address for delivery. I accidentally put my apartment number down, too used to doing that when writing my address, I put '3' and then change it to '8' which is easy to do, the numbers resembling each other, she is in '8' and I put 'Heidi' on the front of the card, I write I hope these put a smile on your face because your smile makes your face beautiful and sign it your Secret Admirer.

I pay for the flowers and walk away and I wonder what the hell I am doing. I do not know this woman, barely spoke to her; I had accused her of being rude. I miss sending flowers to someone; I used to send them to the one I once loved and was going to marry; she would always smile when she got flowers and I loved to see her smile because that meant she wasn't sad and she was sad all the time, she was bi-polar, that's why it never worked, she was always depressed, always believing that things were doomed, nothing would ever work out, she would be a horrible mother, she couldn't have a child with me, but when she had the flowers she would be happy and say thank you and kiss me and act like everything would all right and good from then on.

I think Heidi is sad. She looks sad. I could be projecting. I am aware that this happens to people who are alone. She is alone, she has no one, it is her birthday. But maybe she wants it that way. Maybe she's gotten out of a bad relationship.

Speaking of bad relationships, Lisa has been fighting with this new boyfriend lately, like she used to fight with the rap singer boyfriend, only these fights are less verbal and more physical—twice I have heard them hit each other, scream and yell, and then he runs away, runs down the stairs, and she calls him names and tells him to never come back but he comes back the next day.

The florist across the street from the gas station told me the flowers would be delivered by 3 P.M. This does not happen. I specified that time because I notice Heidi leaves on her bike, which is painted blue, every day around three-thirty and returns around seven-thirty. I have no idea what she does—a part-time job, maybe, or school. I want her to be home so I can hear her reaction.

She does not come home at the time she usually does. There is no one up there. I call the florist but they are closed. I am going to have words with them tomorrow. A woman in a beat-up silver Toyota Corolla pulls into my driveway at 8 P.M. I am about to go out there and tell her not to park in my space; she gets out of the car with a vase of flowers, goes upstairs, knocks on the door. No answer. She leaves the flowers at the door.

I step outside, as if I am going to get my mail from the group of mailboxes on the side of the apartment building. I see the flowers at the door upstairs. The arrangement looks nice. Again, I wonder what the hell I am doing, spending that kind of money on someone I don't know just because she reminds me of someone I once loved and was going to have children with and broke my heart and left me sad.

I almost run up the stairs and take the flowers when I hear some voices that I think are Lisa and her tall boyfriend with tattoos. I go back inside. The voices do not belong to them, but they do come home ten minutes later, with Heidi, and they are giggling happy like they're drunk. They must have taken Heidi somewhere, had food, drinks.

I find myself wishing I had gone with them.

The three walk up the stairs and their giggling stops.

Flowers, Lisa says, are they for me?

Huh, her boyfriend says.

Maybe he thinks her ex, the rapper, sent them.

Ohhhh, Lisa goes, they're for *Heidi*.

What, Heidi says.

For you, Lisa says.

Me.

Your name.

Where did they come from?

They're just here.

This is weird, Heidi goes.

They're very nice, Lisa says.

Cooooool, the boyfriend goes.

What does it say? Lisa asks. The card.

Is this a joke, Heidi says, is someone fucking with my head?

What does the card say? Lisa goes.

Heidi's voice goes: A secret admirer.

Seriously?

The boyfriend with tattoos laughs. I imagine his tattoos laughing.

Weird, Lisa says.

Who would...?

Heidi doesn't finish her sentence.

Well, Lisa says, they *smell* nice.

The boyfriend sneezes, loudly.

Allergies, he goes.

No shit, Lisa says.

***

Two days later, I hear Lisa and the tall boyfriend with tattoos talking on the balcony as they smoke cigarettes:

It's still a mystery, she says.

What is, he says.

The flowers, she says.

Ah, yes, those.

But I think I solved it, she says

Oh.

I think I know who sent them.

Who?

You, she says.

Me?

You, she says.

He laughs at that: Why do you think...?

Because you feel sorry for her, you said you did; you wanted to make her feel good, to be happy on her birthday, 'to smile' like the note said.

Why would I spend money like that on flowers, on her?

Good question. Why would you?

I wouldn't. Not even to be nice.

Tell me the truth, she says.

If I was going to buy flowers for someone, he says, I would buy them *for you.*

That's what I want to hear, Lisa says. Hey, you've *never* gotten me flowers, fucker, she goes.

I'm allergic to them, he tells her.

Right, she says.

He's like, Isn't my dick a good enough present?

Oh, shut up, she goes.

He's like, Didn't you like the box of chocolates?

And she's like, Loved them to the last bite.

So—what *if* I had sent them to her? he goes.

Well, yeah, *what if,* she's like.

Would you be mad?

What do you think, asshole.

Well, it wasn't me, he says.

It's driving her batty, Lisa goes, she can't figure it out, who it is; she's looking at every guy at work and trying to discover clues, the way this guy looks at her or another guy acts around her. She's like, 'What if it's someone I don't want it to be?' Like a married guy, the fat guy, there's this jerk who comes on to every woman at her job, but she doesn't think he would say something romantic like 'I hope these put a smile on your beautiful face.'

He's like, *Is* that romantic?

And she's like, Sure it is.

He goes, Sounds sappy.

It's *kind*, she goes, and *nice*, she says.

He goes, I like the smile on your beautiful face

Quit it, she says, you're just sounding like a jerk, she goes.

I was *trying* to sound romantic, he says.

Not working.

He's like, I *can* be.

And she goes, Ha *ha*. Ha.

He says, You don't think so...

And she goes, Ha ha. *Ha*.

That's an insult, he says.

She goes, Your romance is in your pants.

And he's like, Now you're getting me hot.

✳ ✳ ✳

Sometimes, at night, I can hear Lisa and this boyfriend above me, in their bedroom, having sex. I used to hear her with the other boyfriend. Heidi must hear them too, sleeping in the living room. I wonder if the sounds make her feel the way I do. When I hear Heidi walking around the living room at night, I think this is ridiculous and indeed sad: here are two lonely people, alone, and all that separates them is wood and stucco.

The world never works out the way it should.

***

Two-thirty in the morning: the phone rings and there's no voice, just breathing, the faint sound of a television in the background, tuned to twenty-four hour news, I think.

What is it? I say.

Talk, I say.

You can ask a question, I go.

***

Two weeks later, I see Heidi sitting outside a coffee house, not far from the florist, drinking coffee, eating a bagel, writing or drawing in a blue notebook. I'm getting coffee. She sees me and I see her.

I decide it is time to say hello.

I approach her.

She looks up.

I say, Hi.

She says, Hi.

She closes her notebook but I see, briefly, what she is doing—drawing a vase with flowers.

Can I join you?

She doesn't reply.

I sit across from her.

I say, We're neighbors. I thought I'd say hi.

Why? she asks.

Why not.

Do you want to accuse me of shit again?

Look, I say, that was a mistake.

She smiles.

I didn't mean anything, I say.

I'm kidding, she says, I didn't mean anything.

I tell her my name and she hesitates, and tells me hers. I don't say that I already know it.

We walk to the apartment building together. We don't talk about anything significant, just chitchat between strangers.

Well, I say.

It was nice meeting you, she says.

We're neighbors, I say.

So it seems, she goes.

She walks up the stairs and I go inside. I can hear her walking around up there. I hear her for a while. I take a nap. It's a start, at least.

***

I wake up from my nap to the sounds of violence. Lisa and her tall boyfriend with tattoos are at it again, and it sounds pretty awful—they both scream at each other, throw things at one another, and it sounds like he tosses her against the wall. I hear hands hitting flesh—slaps or punches, who knows, but it does not sound good.

Heidi runs down the stairs and knocks on my door.

Help, she says, can I come in...

I let her in. She's wearing blue and white pajamas, holding her blue notebook. Her feet are bare. Her toenails are painted dark blue.

I just need to be somewhere safe, she says.

Maybe I should call the cops, I say.

No, no, she says, they'll stop soon, they always stop and make nicey-nice.

It sounds bad.

It only sounds that way.

She sits down on the couch. I sit on the floor across from her.

I'm sorry, she says.

It's okay, I say.

The fighting wanes down upstairs, and stops.

There, Heidi says.

How do you, I start to say.

I don't, she says. I don't even like having a roommate but she needed one and I need to save money for something that is coming up.

What's that? I ask.

What?

What's coming up?

She goes, Wouldn't you like to know...

And I'm like, Sorry, didn't mean to pry.

She glares at me.

What's wrong? I ask.

Wrong?

Are you okay?

I know it's you, she goes.

Me, I say.

I know it's *you*, asshole, she says.

She tosses the notebook at me. It is open to the picture of a vase and flowers she has drawn. There are several drawings on other pages, different angles of the flowers, close-ups, pictures of a single flower.

I know it's *you*, she says, no one I know knows where I live.

You draw nice, I say.

You're a *jerk*, she says. You think it's nice, but it's not, 'Secret Admirer.' It makes a girl feel stalked. I was going nuts trying to figure out who would send me flowers, who would say my face is beautiful. I couldn't sleep. I had strange dreams. And it was you all along. Don't deny it. I've seen you *look* at me. And today—*today*.

Your face is beautiful, I say.

Oh fuck you, she says, you don't know what you're talking about. Don't say 'I'm sorry.' That's not what I want to hear. I don't want to hear anything. You have no idea what I've been through. You don't know my life. What do you want from me?

Nothing, I say.

A date? she says. Do you want a date, romance, sex, love?

I wanted you to smile.

Fuck you, she says, fuck your smiles. You have no idea who I am. You have no idea what I've been through.

You're right, I don't.

Lisa and her boyfriend start yelling at each other again.

I'm being a bitch, Heidi says, her voice soft now. Maybe you were trying to be nice. I don't know what you want. You seem nice. It's just—*weird*.

They're at it again, I say.

I'm pregnant, she says.

Excuse me?

I'm eleven weeks pregnant, she says.

I ask, What about the father?

And she's like, Yeah, what about that guy, huh?

Things are getting loud and physical upstairs.

I think I should call the police, I say.

Why? Heidi says.

What if he kills her? I say.

She'll beat him to it. She has a gun.

It's not sounding good, I say.

It sounds worse than it really is.

Sounds like they are hurting each other.

That's what people in love do, she goes, they *hurt* each other.

That's not love, I say.

You saying you know anything about love?

I don't know anything about anything, I say.

She goes, No shit, Mr. Pity Party.

What did I ever do to you? I say. They were just *flowers*. Who hurt you so badly, that you act like this?

She goes, Who hurt you so badly that you make a fool of yourself, sending flowers to a stranger you barely know? And why the hell don't you use your parking space?

What?

Why don't you use your fucking parking space?

I don't have a car.

So let someone else use it.

It's mine, I say.

We have to raise our voices, over the yelling and screaming and hitting upstairs.

It's a waste of a good parking space, Heidi says.

Then park in it, I tell her, it's yours now, all yours.

Jerk, she says. I don't have a car, she goes, I ride a bike, she goes.

I know.

You've been *watching* me.

Park your bike there, I say.

I'm keeping it, she says.

Keep it, then, it's yours, I say.

I meant the baby, she goes, I'm keeping the baby.

Something shatters upstairs—glass, a plate.

I'm going to have it, I won't have an abortion, she says.

Something else shatters up there, and someone gets thrown into a wall.

That's it, I say, and reach for the phone.

So do you think you could fall in love with a pregnant woman who is pregnant with some other guy's child? she asks me.

What did you say?

You heard me.

We both hear a loud sound—a loud pop, a boom. And then another. And then silence.

Heidi and I just look at each other. We are frozen—I am holding the phone and she is touching her slightly protruding belly under her blue pajamas.

Oh my god, she says.

The phone starts to ring but I don't answer it.

I know she is going to have a boy, a son.

Cyclops

There is a one-eyed man in Brooklyn and he wants to save your life. The eye was lost in a freak fishing accident; he was fishing on a lake, a great lake, and he was a boy. There was water everywhere. The shore was beyond his field of vision. A shining hook winked at him, swooped down and took his eye. His uncle screamed, "Oh my fucking God. Your mother is going to kill me, Johnny. Get that fucking thing out of your eye."

There is something about him that is hard to resist. You might even say he's a lady's man. He's a waffle man. He makes the batter that makes the waffle. He's an artist really. I guess I shouldn't be surprised that my wife, Cathy, fell in love with the fellow.

"I'm leaving you," Cathy said one night.

"What?" I said. "What are you telling me?" I said.

"Our marriage," she said, "is over. You know this. You've known this for a long time."

Yes, I did; yes.

"I'm in love with Johnny," she said.

"Who?"

"You know, Johnny."

"The Cyclops?" I said.

"That's *mean*," she said, "that's *horrible*," she said.
"Since when?" I asked.
She said, "Does it matter?"

***

So I went to see the Cyclops. I know it was stupid. Thing was, I used to work at the Waffle House; I also made the batter. I waited until five minutes before closing. I went inside. Johnny the Cyclops looked up with his one eye and said, "Oh you. Why are you here?"

"You know why I'm here," I said.

"What is it?" he said. "Do you want to pick a fight with me?" he said. "Is that it?" he said.

"No," I said.

"Good. I don't want to fight you. I like you," he said.

***

He closed the Waffle House and we sat down and had some beers.

"So," he said.

"So," I said; "you're taking my wife from me."

"It's been over between you and Cathy for some time," he said. "You know this."

Yes, I did; yes.

"How long," I said.

"Does it matter?"

"Yes."

"No it doesn't."

"I think it does," I said.

"The answer will only hurt you," he said, "hurt you more than the pain you already feel," he said, "because I can see it on your face, the way you sit down, the way your body moves, that you're in pain."

I drank some beer.

"It's okay," he said, "I know pain."

"It doesn't matter," I said.

He touched my hand and said, "Listen," he smiled, "listen to me," he said, "give me the opportunity to save your life."

"What's that?"

"I want to invite you to my church."

"You have a church?"

"There's a small church I attend," he said, "and it's wonderful."

"No kidding," I said.

"I kid you not," he said.

"Does Cathy go to this church?"

Johnny smiled and said, "That's where it all began."

"I have no interest in church," I said.

"I never did either, until last year."

"Cathy doesn't even believe in God," I said.

"It's funny how things change," he said.

"Yes it is," I said, and smashed the beer bottle over his head.

He wasn't fazed. There was some blood, but it was like he expected me to do that.

"I understand," he said. "This is okay."

"It's not okay," I said. "Jesus, man, I'm sorry."

He smiled. "I forgive you," he said.

"Don't forgive me," I said. "Kick my ass."

He just smiled at me.

***

Cathy was packing her things in suitcases when I got home.

"I did something bad," I said. "You're going to hate me."

She said, "I could never hate you."

She said, "Johnny called. I *know*."

She said, "*We* know you didn't mean it. Everything is okay."

"What?" I said, and: "What the..."

"Listen," she said, "this is for the best. This is saving my life. It's saving yours. I love the Cyclops."

"What the hell is wrong with you two?" I wanted to yell this but it came out weak and resigned and I hated that.

Aliens

I t's a pretty cold Christmas Eve and I've been sitting at the doorstep of my ex-girlfriend's condo for some time now. I like the way the door feels against my back. I look at a moth flying around the porch light.

Terri finally shows up, holding a grocery bag.

"You," she says.

"Me," I say.

"What are you doing here?" she says.

"It's Christmas Eve," I say.

"So," she says.

"So," I say. "What do you mean 'so'?"

"I could call the police," she says.

"You could."

"I should."

"Why?"

She goes, *"Why* are you here?"

"I'm cold," I say.

"It's not that cold."

"It is when you've been sitting out here for an hour."

"You've been sitting out here for an *hour?"*

"Two hours."

*"God*dammit," she says.

"Don't be mean," I say.

She says, *"Don't* start that shit with me."
"I'm cold," I say; "I'm hungry."
"God*dammit,*" she goes.
"It's Christmas Eve."
She says, *"God*damn you."

***

Her three cats sniff at my feet. My own cats are dead now. Well, one is, having eaten a chicken bone from the garbage; the other went off somewhere and never came back.

"I can't believe I let you in," Terri says, going to the kitchen with her bag. "I almost had a feeling you'd be here anyway. Like a vision or a dream."

"What's in the bag?" I say.

"Pasta," she says, bringing out a bag of dried pasta, and then a jar of sauce.

"Did you get meatballs?"

"Of course."

"I love meatballs," I say. "I can't tell you how much I've been dreaming about a nice home-cooked meal, like the nice home-cooked meals you used to make."

"Are you saying that to pull at my heartstrings?" she says.

"No."

"Yes you are."

"I didn't mean to."

"Yes you did."

I open the fridge and look in—it's a sudden urge.

"Help yourself," Terri says sarcastically.

"Sorry."

"No," she says, "it's okay."

I grab a beer.

"I don't think you should," she says.

"What?" I say.

"You know how you get, sometimes, when you drink."

"And you don't?"

"Well," she says.

"I haven't been drinking like I used to. Not these past months. I've cut back."

"I started drinking more," she goes.

***

We have white wine with our dinner of pasta and meatballs. We sit across from each other at the table.

"You've lost weight," Terri says.

"I haven't been eating like I used to."

"I can tell."

"Am I being rude?"

She smiles. "I like it when you eat food I cook."

"I haven't been working."

"You look pale."

"I've been cold," I say. "No heat."

"*Why* don't you take care of yourself?"

"I can't."

"*Bull*shit."

"I never could."

"All your life you've relied on women to take care of you."

"You make it sound so bad."

"Not *every* woman can play Mommy."

We don't talk for a while. We eat and drink.

Terri says, "Christmas doesn't mean anything to me. It's just another day. People put too much into it."

"Is that what your step-father made you believe?"

"How can you say something so mean?"

"Christmas is dreaming about all those toys and good things," I say. "Happiness and smiles."

'That's for children," she says.

***

"You were right," Terri says as we put the dinner dishes in the sink, "what you said."

"What did I say?"

"About my step-father."

"Oh."

She says, "He had to take the magic out of everything, the bastard." She asks, "You want to hear about this dream I had?"

"What dream?"

"I told you I had a feeling you'd be at my door tonight, right? Right. Well, I had this dream the other night—"

"Okay."

She says, "I dreamt you were there, in the cold, just like you were, and I let you in. The thing is, you weren't you. You were an alien. Well, not an alien, but an alien had taken over your body. This alien informed me of this. You were sick or something, you weren't well, you were going to die, and the alien couldn't stay in your body."

"How did it take over my body?"

"I don't know. The alien didn't have a body, it was non-corporeal or something. This doesn't matter, it was a dream, not an episode of *The Twilight Zone*. The alien wanted my body, you see. It wanted to jump from your body to mine. I told it I couldn't do that. I wanted to be with you. So this is what it did: it took my soul out of my body and put it in your body, with you, then stole my body. So there the two of us were: our souls stuck in your body. The tragic thing was that you were dying, so we were doomed to die together."

"I want to kiss you," I say.

She turns her face.

"You can kiss me on the cheek," she says, and I do. "Hey, do you want to watch TV?" she says.

⁂

"Are you going to sleep here?" Terri asks after the movie on TV.

"What?"

"I guess that's a yes."

"It's cold at home."

I get up, she pushes me back on the couch.

"I'll get you some bedding," she says.

She leaves and returns with a blanket and two big pillows.

"Terri."

"What?" she says. "You didn't think you were going to sleep in my bed, did you?"

"I was hoping."

"And do what?" she says. "Did you think you were going to fuck me?"

"I was hoping I could kiss you."

"Kiss me?"

"I was hoping I could hug you."

"Hug the extra pillow. That's why I got it. You like pillows. They're big and warm."

"I like pillows," I say.

"You can kiss me goodnight," she says, after a moment.

"On the lips?"

"That's what kisses are for."

I kiss her on the lips. I kiss her again. I try a third time, but she moves away.

"I'm sure the cats will sleep on top of you, like they always used to."

"They miss me."

"They do."

She leaves to her bedroom.

I lie on the couch, with my two pillows, and cover myself with the blanket. Only one of her cats stays with me, the other two follow her.

Adventure

Phone Call

I got the phone call while I was watching television. *Star Trek.* I think I could've been watching too much television.

"Hello," I said.

"Hello," a woman's voice said, "who is this?"

"Who are you?" I asked.

"Andrea," she said.

"Do I know you?"

"I don't think so," she said. "I found your phone number. I was curious. I was angry. I called. I'm sorry."

Angry? "I don't understand."

"I live in San Diego," she said. "My husband's name is Barry Redman. Do you know him?"

"No," I said.

"I found your phone number on the back of a matchbook," she told me. "The matchbook was from a bar. The matchbook was in the jacket pocket of my husband's gray suit, which he was wearing two nights ago. He was out late. He came home drunk."

"Is this some kind of weird joke?" I said. "Did Lisa put you up to this?"

"Lisa?"

"My wife."

"I don't know a Lisa."

"I don't know a Barry Redman."

"Where is your wife now?"

"Is this a joke?"

"I'm sorry," she said, and hung up.

I went back to the television.

I love *Star Trek*.

Lisa

Lisa called later that night. She'd had a few drinks. She likes to drink, and so do I. It's the one thing we immediately had in common when we met seven years ago. She was down in San Diego still, on business for the company she worked for. She'd been in San Diego for five days. This was her last night. "I can't wait to get back home," she said.

"I got the strangest telephone call today," I said.

"What?"

"It was," I said. "I don't know," I said, "it was nothing."

"I'm beat," Lisa said.

The next afternoon, I drove to the airport and picked her up. We kissed and didn't talk. We went home. From the corner of my eye, I kept looking at her, to see if she were different.

Home, I made us two vodka tonics and we sat in front of the television. The television wasn't on. No *Star Trek* re-runs.

"Do you know someone named Barry Redman?" I asked.

Lisa was about to take a drink. She stopped.

"What?" she said.

"Barry Redman," I said.

"Why do you ask?"

"I got a funny phone call yesterday," I said. "A woman called. She was in San Diego. Said she found our number on a matchbook from a bar. Her husband's name is—"

"Yes," Lisa said, "I know him."

"A business associate?" I asked.

"No," she said.

"A friend?" I asked.

"I don't know him that well, *really*," she said.

The Truth

We didn't make love when we went to bed. She didn't seem to be in the mood and I wasn't either.

"So who is Barry Redman?" I asked.

She didn't answer. She lay there, back turned to me.

"Lisa?" I said.

"*What*," she said. She sat up, looking at me. She pulled the sheets across her breasts. "What the fuck do you *want?*" she said. "What do you want me to say?"

"I don't know," I said.

"What the *fuck* do you want me to say?" She was crying now. "You want the truth? Okay. I'll tell you the *truth*. Barry Redman is someone I met at a bar in San Diego. A—a man."

"Oh," I said. I got up, went to the bathroom. I didn't have to pee. I looked at myself in the mirror. I put on my robe and went back to the bedroom. Lisa was on the bed, looking at the ceiling.

"Why did you give him our number?" I asked.

"I don't know," she said. "I don't know what I was thinking. Like I could *really* take a call here. I must've meant to give him my pager number and and *and*, I don't know. *I was drunk.* I was really drunk."

"Did you fuck him?"

She still looked at the ceiling.

I approached the bed.

"Lisa," I said, "did you fuck him?"

She sat up.

"No," she said. "I wanted to. But I didn't."

"Oh," I said.

"I sucked his cock," she said, looking at me.

I went to the kitchen.

I made some drinks.

I fell asleep in front of the television. Tony Robbins infomercials: how to improve your life and get rich.

Hashbrowns & Eggs

Woke up to the smell of food. Lisa was making breakfast in the kitchen. She wore a t-shirt and shorts.

"Do you want hashbrowns with your eggs?"

"You sucked his cock?" I asked.

"Yes," she said.

"Why?"

"Why?" she said. "Don't ask dumb questions," she said.

"Did he come in your mouth?"

"Yes," she said.

"Just like that?"

"People come."

"You didn't make him wear a condom?"

"I don't like the taste of latex."

"That's dangerous," I said.

"He seemed pretty safe," she said.

I sat down.

"What did I do?" I asked.

"You didn't *do* anything," Lisa said. She didn't look at me. "Our marriage has dulled. You know that. There's no—excitement. I'm a bad person, I know. We have a good marriage."

"Have there been others?"

"Yes."

"How many?"

"I won't answer that," she said.

"How many?"

"I guess I should pack some stuff," she said.

Second Phone Call

The phone rang while I was watching television. It was the news. Bill O'Reilly on Fox.

"Hello," the woman's voice said. "I called the other day. From San Diego."

"Andrea Redman?"

"Yes," she said. "I need to talk to you."

"Your husband met my wife at a bar," I said.

"I know," she said. "He told me. He said they didn't sleep together."

"No," I said, "Lisa only gave him a blowjob."

"What?"

"You know what a blowjob is?"

"I *know* what it is," she said. "I don't believe it."

"That's what my wife told me," I said. "She's gone now."

"With Barry?"

"They hardly know each other," I said, "I doubt they have anything romantic going on," I said.

Silence.

"I shouldn't be surprised," Andrea Redman said. "He's done this before. I'd hoped it stopped."

"Ask him what it was like," I said.

"What?"

"What it was like," I said, "getting his dick blown by my wife."

She hung up.

Lisa's Call

Lisa called me from a hotel room. "What should we do?" she asked.

"What will *you* do?"

"I'm not sure what to do," she said. "Do you want a divorce?"

"I'm not sure."

"I love you," she said, "no matter what."

"I want to know how many?"

"Is it important?"

"Yes," I said.

"Six," she said, "I think. But they didn't mean anything."

I hung up.

Los Angeles

Andrea Redman called in the afternoon.

"I thought you might call," I said.

"I'm in L.A.," she said.

"Why are you in L.A.?"

"It's only a two hour drive up," she said. "I was hoping—I was hoping maybe you'd meet me."

"Okay," I said.

She arrived forty minutes later. I watched for her. She drove a small station wagon. She was tall and slim, with short blonde hair and a thin face, too gaunt. Maybe it was the glasses she wore. She rang the door bell and I answered.

"Andrea Redman, I presume."

"Hello."

"Did you find my house okay?"

"I got lost once, but I'm here."

Coffee

I offered her some coffee. She said that'd be nice. I got us both a cup of coffee and we sat in the living room. The television was on, sound off. We sat there quietly, sipping coffee.

"Well," I said.

"Well," she said. "I don't know what to say. I was rehearsing all kinds of things in my head on the way down here. My mind is blank now."

"Relax."

"I *am* relaxed. I just can't *think*. I don't know why I'm here. I got into my car and started to drive. I thought you had some answers. I don't know what the questions are. I woke up this morning and my husband was gone. I don't know where he is."

She added, "I wasn't surprised."

"I don't think he's in L.A," I said.

"No," she said.

"But you are," I said.

"Yes," she said.

I looked out the window.

"Listen," I said. "It's starting to get dark out. You want to go to a bar, or something?"

"Sure," Andrea Redman said. "Or something."

Tequila Tonics

We took her car. We went to a little bar I like, one Lisa and I used to go to. We'd been here last week. Andrea and I sat at the counter. "What would you like?" I asked.

"It doesn't matter," she said. "Whatever you're having," she said.

I ordered two tequila tonics.

"Strong," she said.

I drank mine fast, and ordered another.

"I'm not much of a drinker," she said. "Barry likes to drink."

"Lisa likes to drink," I said. "I do too."

"I should take up drinking more."

"Wouldn't hurt."

We sat there.

"Do we have anything to talk about?" I asked.

"I don't know," she said. "I feel uncomfortable."

"I'm sorry," I said.

"It's not *you*," she said, taking her glasses off and putting them back on. "It's this bar. I never feel comfortable in dark bars," she said.

Beer

We left the bar and picked up a six-pack of beer from the liquor store. I told her where to drive, near Santa Monica. I told her where to park.

"It's peaceful here," I said, opening two beers.

"I like the sound of the waves," Andrea Redman said. "We don't live near the beach. I always wanted to live by the beach," she said, drinking beer. "This is good beer. I usually don't drink beer. If I drink at all, it's wine. Not a lot of wine, a glass, two at the most," she said.

"When I drink wine," I said, "my eyes itch like crazy the next morning."

"I keep trying to picture them together," she said. "But I can't. I don't know what your wife looks like."

"I have a photo," I said, taking out my wallet.

"I do too." She opened her purse. "Barry."

We exchanged photos.

"Oh," she said, giving my wallet back. "I still can't see them together. Can you?"

"I don't know."

"He swore they didn't make love."

"He just got his cock sucked."

"If he wanted that, why didn't he ask me?" She drank her beer. "I give him that when he wants it." She drank her beer and looked at me. "Would you like me to show you? Would you like me to suck you?"

"Yes," I said.

"Okay," she said, "take it out."

I unzipped my pants.

Andrea finished her beer. She looked at me holding it. She bent down. I barely felt her mouth graze me. She came back up, adjusting her glasses.

"I can't," she said.

"It's okay," I said.

Motel Room

We got a motel room, near the beach. There was a bar connected to the motel so we went there. She was getting drunk. "I want to get *really* drunk," she said, and I had no problem with that. There were mostly men in the bar, as bars go. I ordered us two drinks and we sat in a booth. "I think I can go through with this," Andrea said, kissing me on the mouth.

A man with a thick mustache joined us in our booth. He was heavy-set and smiling.

"Hello," he said, "I'm Rick."

"Hello," Andrea said.

"Can I join you?"

"No," I said.

"There's this joke I want to tell you both," he said.

"A joke?" Andrea said.

"Yeah," Rick said, "but now I can't remember it. I think I drank too much."

"Haven't we all," Andrea said, and giggled.

"You're cute," Rick said. "I mean, gorgeous. The both of you. All hugs and kisses. Like you're on some adventure. I envy you."

"Thanks," I said, "but we'd like to be left alone. We were having a private conversation."

"Yeah," Rick said. Something changed in him. "What's so private about it, huh? *Tell me.* What's so god-damned *private* about it?"

"Would you please leave," I said.

"What're you gonna *do* about it?"

Andrea laughed.

Rick looked down. "I'm sorry. I'm just drunk. I haven't been with a woman in over a year. When I see a pretty woman . . ."

He got up and left.

"That was strange," Andrea said.

Surprise Visit

Back in the motel room, we started to kiss and undress. There was a knock on the door. Andrea went to get it, stumbling, wearing only her skirt and bra.

"Ignore it," I said.

"Maybe it's room service," she said.

"Motels don't have that," I said.

I don't know what she was thinking. She opened the door, half-naked, and said, "Surprise!" She was laughing, until a hand shoved her back. She collapsed on the floor, glasses falling off her face.

Before I could move, Rick was in the room. He shut the door. He held a black revolver.

"Hello again," he said.

"Oh boy," I said.

"I had to do this," he said. "This is what's gonna happen. I'm robbing you, because I've been out of work longer than I want to remember and I need money. Then I'm gonna fuck your lady friend because I haven't been with a woman for a while."

Andrea just stared at him.

"Don't make this difficult," Rick said. "This can be fun if you'd like," he said.

I rushed Rick. He wasn't expecting it. I slapped the gun out of his hand, and hit him a few times in the face. He went down. It was all a silly drunk moment and probably would've been funny under different circumstances.

"Are you crazy?" Andrea said. "He could've *shot* us!"

"No." I picked up the gun. "It's fake."

"How can you tell?"

"You look at a revolver, you can see bullets in the chamber. This is a fake chamber. The whole thing is fake."

"*Oh,*" Andrea said, picking up her glasses.

Coffee and Pancakes

We sat in a diner that was near-by, eating pancakes, drinking coffee, getting sober. We'd left Rick in the motel room bed; he seemed to be sleeping well.

"I guess I should go home now," Andrea said.

"Can you drive?"

"Yes. I need to go home. I've had enough excitement to last me the year, my life. Barry is probably wondering. Maybe he's even worried. I've never stayed away from home before."

"What will you tell him?"

"I don't have to tell him anything."

"Are you staying with him?"

"Yes," she said, "he's my husband."

6 A.M.

Andrea drove me home. I wanted to kiss her goodbye. We smiled at each other, and that was enough. It was 6 A.M. Lisa's car was there. She was in the bedroom, packing. We looked at each other. I went to the kitchen and made myself a vodka tonic.

Lisa followed.

"Just came by to get more of my stuff," she said. "I have to look for an apartment today."

"Don't," I said. "Don't."

Lisa came to me then, putting her head against my chest, and I held her.

"Lisa," I said.

She said nothing.

Looking for Wanda Beyond the Salton Sea

1.

Angry words: they're fighting.

In the car, they are fighting.

Outside the Salton Sea, they yell at each other:

Bastard!

Cunt!

Asshole!

Bitch!

Motherfucker!

Cocksucker!

Whorepipe!

Jerk!

David and Wanda: married, mid-30s, married for five years, and now it seems to be over.

They have left Borrego Springs.

Borrego Springs: they thought the love would re-kindle; the silence would make them happy; that all the bad things of the marriage would go away.

No. No, this did not happen.

They're driving back to Los Angeles, by way of the Salton Sea, to Indio, to Palm Springs and then L.A.

In L.A., Wanda says: I want a divorce.

Whatever, David says.

What-*evah*, she goes, and: Don't ever call me a whorepipe again, you asspipe.

She laughs.

He does not laugh.

He says, I need a drink.

You *always* need a drink, she says, and: I need some *sleep*. I could sleep for a week, a month, a year, and maybe when I woke up you'd be gone and it'd be like we never met.

Where they met: Borrego Springs.

Borrego Springs is not the answer to their problems.

Their problems are bigger than Borrego Springs.

2.

David: behind the wheel. Driving fast.

Slows down outside Salton City.

He spots a liquor store: just what he was looking for.

That's the ticket, he says.

He needs at least a twelve pack of beer and a pint of vodka to drink on the drive to L.A. with his angry wife sitting next to him.

He parks in the parking lot.

Drink and drive, Wanda says, go ahead and put our lives in danger.

I'm the designated drinker, he says.

Funny, she says.

You want something? he asks.

I want a lot of things, she says.

To drink? Eat?

No.

No?

No, she goes.

No, he says.

Jesus, she says, and hey, she goes, those guys give me the creeps, they're staring at us.

David looks: three deeply tanned, or naturally brown, bums hanging outside the liquor store. One sits in a plastic lawn chair, one leans against the wall, one is spinning in circles and looking up at the clear blue sky of the California desert.

None of them wear shoes. Their bare feet are covered in dirt and mud. Their clothes are soiled by dirt and mud and old beer stains, piss stains, puke stains. They all have gray or white hair, in their 50s; their teeth yellow and crooked.

Their eyes: bloodshot.

Two of them stare at David and Wanda with those bloodshot eyes.

The spinning man stops spinning and looks at them too.

Let's get out of here, Wanda says.

I'll be quick, David says.

She goes, Those men are *weird*.

They think *we're* weird because we're strangers, outsiders, we don't belong in Salton City; we're not from here.

We don 't belong anywhere, she says, don't you get it?

Come inside with me, he says.

I don't want to, she says.

Whatever.

What-*evah*.

3.

He walks by the three men and they smell something bad: sweat and dirt and piss and bad breath. He nods at them. They stare and say nothing.

Wanda sticks out her tongue.

Inside the liquor store, David buys a twelve-pack of Heineken and a small bottle of vodka. He uses his credit card. He is only gone two, three minutes.

Outside, Wanda is not in the car. He walks by the three men who smell something bad and they snicker and giggle.

He looks at them: what?

They laugh loudly, shaking their heads, pointing at him, pointing at his car.

What? he goes.

He looks around.

Where is his wife, his goddamn wife, where is Wanda?

Wanda? he goes, and: Wanda?

There's no restroom here, so she didn't leave to piss. He puts the bags in the car. Her purse is gone. One of her shoes is on the floor.

He goes, Wanda?

He walks over to the three men who smell something bad like swear and dirt and piss and bad breath and he asks, Did you gentleman happen to see where my wife went?

They laugh.

The woman in the car, he says.

They laugh.

In the car, he says, his voice louder, you guys are right here, I know you saw where my wife went. Her name is Wanda.

They laugh.

He goes, What's *wrong* with you?

They laugh.

They don't speak English, a voice says.

The voice: belongs to a man wearing a cowboy hat, walks around from the other side of the store. Chewing something, tobacco or gum. In his forties, unshaven, too many lines on his face for a man that age.

What *do* they speak? David says.

The man with the cowboy hat shrugs and goes, Not sure; not English.

Well, did you see where my wife went?

Wife?

She was sitting in the car.

That so?

This isn't like her.

Like who?

My wife.

Wife?

Wanda, yes, wife, he says; and he's annoyed.

Hmm, the man in the hat goes.

Did you? David says.

Did I what?

See her?

A woman?

Yes, she's a *woman.*

The man goes, Haven't seen a woman around here. They're usually a rare catch—sight, you know. I mean, you out of town types with your nice fancy car and all. I mean, who the hell comes out to the Salton Sea when they come to the great outdoors?

We were just passing through, David says.

You all do, the man says.

4.

Sheriff deputy says, Can't file a missing person's report until after twenty-four hours, I'm afraid. That's the rules; that's the law.

The deputy is just a kid, no more than twenty-two, twenty-three years old, smooth tan face, even white teeth, sparkling green eyes. David wonders when he got so old.

It's 111 degrees out, David says, she has no water, she can't be safe in this heat, not after two hours.

I'm sorry, says the deputy. Come tomorrow, eh.

Tomorrow?

Best we can do.

The three smelly tanned men laugh.

Do you know who they are? David asks the deputy.

Yes.

Who are they?

Local bodies.

They were here, they *had* to see where my wife went, David says.

I'll ask them.

The deputy walks over and talks to the three smelly dirty men for a moment. Their voices are low.

The three men shake their heads.

The deputy walks back to David.

They didn't see anything, the deputy says.

Bullshit, David says.

That's what they tell me.

What the hell am I supposed to do?

Wait.

Wait for what?

To see if she comes back, the deputy says.

Where? Here?

Motel down that way.

Motel, David says.

Or you can go back to Borrego Springs and wait, the deputy says. You think maybe she went back there?

To Borrego?

Perhaps.

How? On foot?

The deputy shrugs and goes, Or hitched a ride. People do that.

Wanda is not the hitching type.

You never know when people change, they do it suddenly.

Oh, you've seen this? David asks.

I've seen some things, the deputy says.

Why would she want to go back to Borrego? David says.

You tell me, the deputy says.

5.

In the motel room in Salton City: David drinks. He doesn't know what else to do but drink. He drinks until things go very black, like he always does.

Nothing changes for him.

6.

Behind the wheel: he drives.

He drives toward the outskirts of the Salton Sea and arrives in a town called Bombay Beach. An old VW bus sits halfway in a pool of sludge.

It smells like the end of the world here.

He has a terrible hangover, again. He walks into the only bar in town—the Sky Lodge—to help with the hangover. A couple of beers and a couple of shots should do the trick.

There are half a dozen men and women in the bar. They are all in their sixties and have leathery, tanned skin. They have bored eyes. Their heads turn and stare at him,

They stare at him like he's a meteorite that fell from the heavens.

He is a stranger.

They are not used to strangers.

He nods at them but they do not nod back.

David sits at the bar counter and orders a draft mug and a shot of tequila. That goes down fast. He orders another mug and a shot of vodka.

Later, he's ordering whiskey straight.

Has anyone seen my wife? he says a few hours later, loud and belligerent.

Her name is Wanda, have you seen her?! he goes.

And he goes: Don't any of you dead people know anything?!?

7.

Asleep: in his car.

On the side of the road.

He opens his eyes at two in the morning and sees a lot of stars in the desert sky. Something whizzes by in the air, a bright light shaped like a saucer.

Aliens, he mutters. UFOs and aliens.

Maybe she was abducted by aliens.

One story is as good as another.

8.

From town to town, bar to bar, he drinks and asks questions. He says he is looking for his wife. No one knows a Wanda, has seen a Wanda.

He gets drunk and angry.

Maybe she doesn't exist, a bartender says just before David is 86'ed out.

What? What's that? David goes.

Maybe you made her up, says the bartender, I mean, really, dude, what kind of woman would want to be with a loudmouth asshole like you?

9.

The town of Indio.

David: in a motel room.

Outside are date trees.

He looks at the TV and gets drunk, a twelve-pack of beer and a fifth of bourbon.

Maybe I made her up, he says.

10.

It happens in Palm Springs.

After a night of looking around and asking about his wife—who may or may not be real—David goes to sleep in his motel room and two hours later, four men burst into the room, wake him up, slap him around, punch him, beat him, and tell him to stop his quest.

He knows his attackers, he has seen them before: at

the Salton Sea.

The man in the cowboy hat and the three smelly men with tanned skin.

Only two of the smelly men hit him with their fists. The third stands in a corner and spins round in circles and laughs.

The man with the cowboy hat also hits him.

David is in pain, a lot of pain.

Too much pain.

His eyes are swollen, his lip cut in several places, a few teeth are loose.

He is on the floor, curled up like a fetus.

The spinning man stops spinning and makes his way over to David and kicks David several times in the chest.

There is the sound of something cracking.

And more pain.

The man in the cowboy hat bends down and looks at David.

The man in the hat says, Forget Wanda. Stop looking for her, stop asking about her. It's over. She's ours now.

He tries to talk.

We have your wife now, he says, and we have many plans for that hot piece of ass.

11.

David drives.

He drives back to Los Angeles.

It's not easy to do this: all the pain from the beating and what he knows must be two cracked ribs.

Three teeth are missing from his mouth.

He thought of going back to the Salton Sea and telling the deputy what happened, that those horrid men kidnapped his wife and were doing god-knows-what to her, but he has a notion that the deputy might be in on it.

He will go to L.A. and contact someone in the FBI.

He will get his wife back, even though he hates her.

He missed her.

Maybe I am free now, he thinks.

Maybe he won't go to the FBI.

No, he has to save her.

He has to save something in this marriage.

12.

She's home.

David walks into the house in West Hollywood, where he and Wanda have lived for five years, and he hears music on the stereo system and finds Wanda sitting in the living room, sipping a glass of pinot grigio and reading the latest issue of *Harper's*.

She looks up at him.

Wanda, he says.

What happened to you? she says.

What happened to *me?*

You look a mess. Did someone kick your ass?

What happened to *you?* At the Salton Sea, he goes.

Does it matter?

What the fuck, he goes.

Don't start, she goes.

Those men, he goes.

Didn't you get the *message*, David?

He thinks about it.

Now he understands.

He goes, Message received.

We'll get lawyers, she says, we'll be civilized about this.

He says, Of course.

Do you need to see a doctor? I think you should.

I will tomorrow.

Would you like a glass of wine? she offers.

I would, he replies.

I'll pour it for you, she says.

He says, Thanks.

He means it.

The Birds

There were seven dead birds on the porch when I opened up the house after being away for three months. This is what happens when things rely on me for survival. I decided to leave the bodies. I was just here to collect memories into suitcases. The phone kept ringing and ringing. I didn't answer it. Before I left, I took one of the dead birds, placing it carefully in the smaller suitcase.

Baby Brother

Nicole's baby brother's first word was a name for her—her baby brother called her "Gagol." She didn't like it. "I thought they were supposed to say something like 'Da-da' or 'Ma-ma,' not 'Gagol,' " she said. Her parents, her daddy and mommy, were too busy working, always away from home, to notice or care.

"Gagol Gagol Gagol!" Nicole's baby brother said over and over, laughing and hopping about like 18-month old babies like to do.

"I hate that," Nicole said. "Stop," Nicole said.

Nicole's boyfriend, a nice young fellow with glasses, said, "Kind of sounds like Gogol." He said, "Cool."

"Who? What?" said Nicole.

"Gogol," her boyfriend said, "a great Russian writer."

"Whatever," she said, "I wish he would call me something else."

Nicole's boyfriend was seventeen and was always reading this book or that. He was getting a comparative literature scholarship at some big university in the Midwest, based on an essay he wrote that Nicole tried to read but did not understand.

"Gagol!" said her baby brother in his sleep.

It was summer. Nicole had turned fifteen to six-
teen that summer. She was given the task to look after her
baby brother all summer long, cutting the family expenses
down since her parents didn't have to hire a babysitter or
put the baby in baby daycare.

Nicole didn't mind. What else would she do during the summer? Her boyfriend would come over and help
her watch the baby brother, and when the baby brother
took his necessary naps during the day, Nicole and her
boyfriend were able to retreat to her bedroom and have
sex. Sometimes they did it on the couch, watching TV, or
she would sneak in a blowjob when the baby brother was
preoccupied with the things that babies find interesting,
such as dust in a corner or birds in a tree. One time she
had sex with her boyfriend in the shower but she didn't
like it that much: too much water too close to their bodies.

When he wasn't reading a book, she would have
sex with him because that's all there was to do, and she
didn't read books.

She was worried she would miss sex when he left
to that university.

She would simply have to find another boy to have
sex with.

They were having sex the day there was a car ac
cident in front of the house. Two speeding cars. Nicole
wasn't sure what, exactly, happened, other than the two
cars collided into one another and people were hurt.

There was a woman, in her 30s, lying on the ground.
She was bleeding badly, all over her body, cuts from bro-
ken glass. She choked on her own blood, the sound went
gurgle gurgle gurgle.

Nicole and her boyfriend witnessed all this blood
because, upon hearing the cars smash into one another,

they stopped having sex, got dressed, and ran outside to look at what happened.

She and her boyfriend were not the only ones. Everyone in the neighborhood came out to take a look.

"Someone call 911," someone said.

"I did already," someone said.

Nicole watched the woman choke on her blood and then watched the woman stop choking on her blood. The woman was not breathing anymore. Nicole grabbed onto her boyfriend and said, "Oh," and "oh."

Nicole did not notice that her baby brother had walked out of the house to join the crowd. Her baby brother walked up to the woman who was bleeding and not breathing. Her baby brother looked at the woman with curiosity.

"Someone get that baby away from her," someone said.

Sirens were getting closer.

The baby brother leaned down and touched the woman and said, "Gagol."

The woman coughed up an enormous amount of blood and sat up. She looked around.

The crowd took one step back.

"Gagol," said Nicole's baby brother.

"Where am I?" said the woman.

"She's alive!" someone said.

"It's a miracle!" someone else said.

"Oh brother," Nicole said. She was thinking about what her parents would say, do, react.

"Cool," her boyfriend said.

"Gagol," her baby brother said.

Daddy

He's in the hospital with a lot of things stuck in his arms, nodes pasted to his chest, tubes going into his nostrils and mouth. He has been staring at the TV for hours.

"Daddy," his daughter says, "Daddy," she says, "I'm worried."

He looks at her. She is nineteen. She is in college. She is really his step-daughter, not his blood, but he married her mother when she was two years old. He is the only father she has ever known.

"I don't know what to do," she says.

"I was never prepared for something like this," she says.

"I wish Mom was still alive," she says, "she would know what to do."

He wants to tell her that his dead wife, her dead mother, would not know what to do. She would cry, cry and pray to the baby Jesus. "Give me guidance, O Baby Jesus," she would say.

She has been up in Heaven with the baby Jesus for six years now.

His daughter starts to cry, just like her mother. He thinks how much she looks like her mother these days, especially with all those tears.

"You can't die," she says.

"I don't know what to do," she says.

"I don't want to be all alone," she says, "I'm scared of being alone."

He looks at the TV.

"Daddy," she says, "I'm pregnant."

He looks at her and tries to say something.

"That's a lie, I lied," she says, "I just wanted to see if you're paying attention, if you understand, if your mind is here with me, because all you do is stare at that stupid TV."

The color on the TV is too bright. It needs to be adjusted. He wishes he could tell her this, so she would get up and fix the TV. The color hurts his eyeballs.

"But if you die," she says, "I *will* get pregnant. I'll go out and get knocked up so you can have a body to reincarnate in," she says.

"I'm serious about this," she says.

"If you die," she says, "I'll have a baby and that baby will be you and we'll be together. I won't be alone. Then I'll have another baby, so Mom's soul can reincarnate in that one, and the three of us can be a family again."

He looks at the TV.

"Daddy," she says, "this is the perfect plan," she says.

"I feel better now," she says.

"I'm not as scared now," she says. "I know I won't be alone after all."

Last Visit

In uniform, medals and all, I went to the hospital during visiting hours and bought flowers and went to her room where she was lying on the bed, her head bald from the chemotherapy, and said, Hello.

She said, What are you doing here?

She was weak but managed to toss a pillow at me and say, What the hell do you think you're doing here?

She looked fifty years old, not thirty-eight.

Her daughter sat in a chair and said, I called him and asked him to.

What? *Why?* Why the *hell* would you do that?

I want you two to finally make peace, the daughter said.

The daughter is tall, maybe six feet, long blonde hair and small blue eyes.

I have not seen her in seven years, when she was much shorter.

You've grown, I said.

Thank you for coming, she said.

The daughter's mother said, I can't believe you *did this* to me.

The daughter's mother finds a black woolen cap and puts it on her head.

I'm here for peace, I said.

The fuck you are, she said.

Mom, said the daughter, *look* at you, after all this, don't you think it's time to make amends?

I have nothing to say I'm sorry about, the mother said; not to him, she said, *never to him*, she said.

A lot of it was your fault, the daughter said.

How dare you, the mother said.

And a lot of it was mine, I said.

Seven years of this, the daughter said. Enough already! What happened *happened*. Seven years, she said, is a long time to be angry.

An eternity, if it has to be, the mother said.

Mom, the daughter said, you're dying.

Thanks for reminding me, the mother said.

Don't leave this earth with bad mojo lingering, the daughter said.

If there's any mojo, *he* put it there, the mother said, and she pointed a weak finger at me.

I can put all that away, if you can, I said.

Ha! said the mother. Aren't *you* the artist? she asked.

I brought the flowers to her, put them on the bed stand.

I said, This can be a start.

She swung her arm and knocked the flowers to the floor and said, *This* is what I think of your *starts!* Get out of here before I scream, get out of here before I call security, get out of here before I have you arrested!

Mom! said the daughter.

Don't *you* turn against me too! said the mother.

It's useless, I said, it's hopeless.

I know, the daughter said.

Get out, the mother said, just get *out.*

***

That night, in the motel room, we took a shower together after making love. We kissed like we had never kissed be-fore—like it was seven years ago, before I was shipped off to the war in the desert and the artist inside me died.

She'll never forgive us, the daughter said.

I said, It's the way she is, the way she always has been.

She has no peace in her heart, the daughter said.

She never understood, I said.

Would anyone? the daughter said.

Give Me the Gun, He Says

She has his gun, she found it under the bed, and she says she is going to shoot herself, she is going to blow her brains out.

Why would you want to do that? he asks.

I want to die, she says.

Take your meds, he says, take your pills and you'll feel better.

I feel awful, she says, and I want to die right now.

She waves the gun in front of her face, peering into the barrel.

Give me the gun, he says.

You love someone else, she says.

I don't love her, he says.

You're sleeping with her, she says.

That's not the issue, he says.

It's the subscription, she says.

She puts the gun to her head.

Please give me the gun, he says, please.

Stop seeing her and I will, she says.

That's not the point, he says.

Maybe I should shoot her, she says, maybe I should kill her. She can die instead of me.

I give up, he says, go ahead, shoot yourself.

What, she says.

Die, he says, now.

She hands him the gun.

You mean that, she says.

He holds the gun, looks at the gun. He points the gun at her forehead.

Okay, do it, she says. She closes her eyes and says, Just pull the trigger and go to her and you two can live happily ever after in bliss.

There are no bullets, he says.

She opens her eyes.

Bullets, she says.

This gun has no bullets in it, he says.

Goddammit, she says; I can't do *anything* right.

He gets a box of bullets from under the bed and loads the gun and shoots her in the foot. She yells out in pain and her foot is bleeding all over the place.

See how it feels, he says.

That was a lie. That does not really happen. He thinks about doing it. He has the fantasy. It would teach her a lesson.

What really happens is this.

He takes the gun and leaves.

He takes the gun and leaves and never comes back.

He takes the gun and leaves and never comes back and never thinks about her except around 3 A.M. when he can't sleep and he wonders what she is doing, if she has found a new boyfriend, if he made the right decision to be with the woman who sleeps soundly next to him while he has insomnia and replays events of his past inside his mind.

Forbidden Scenes of Affection

"Don't touch me there," she said, but I did, I touched her there, and Helen said again, "I don't want you to touch me there," and I said I did, I wanted to, wanted my hand there more than anything the moment could give. I wanted to feel the beginnings of life. She blushed—her pink skin—her blue eyes looking at the bedroom wall. "Okay," she said. "If you really want to." I put my hand softly, firmly, on her belly, just a slight protrusion, hardly noticeable, her stomach hard, an outie belly-button. Helen sighed, closed her eyes. I wondered what she was seeing behind those lids, wanted inside her dreams. She said, "It's funny to think something is actually growing inside me, there's a life in there."

She was pregnant, twelve weeks pregnant, but it was not my baby, it could never be mine, I'd only known her for two weeks. It was her husband's child, she never let me forget this. The husband she lived with—I'll be with him forever, she'd told me, but I'll never be faithful because I love men too much.

"I want you," I told her, my hand going down her stomach, down farther.

She still looked at the wall; she closed her legs together and said, "How could you want to make love to me?"

This had never been a problem before. She was here with me two days ago, and our love was frantic and fatal. Each time was like the last time we'd ever see each other, blah blah blah. She was the married woman, and everything was up to her.

I said, "I don't understand."

She said, "You never will."

I kissed her and she smiled, and relaxed under me.

I thought what an odd scene this was. From the outside, there was nothing wrong with a man and woman, naked, lying on a bed. But when you got the details, the scene became distorted, if not grotesque.

"I'm pregnant," she said, "and you still want me?"

"Yes," I said.

"This won't last," she said. "I just want you to know."

"I know."

But it lasted longer than either of us probably thought. She came over at least once a week, sometimes twice. Helen told me she couldn't stay away and she didn't know why. I only smiled and kissed her. She would touch her belly and say, "Look at me, do you still want me?"

I said, "Yes, yes, yes," and held her, and took her to the bed.

Her breasts got heavier, filled with milk. I liked to touch them, although I had to do it gently; she said they were quite sensitive.

She was six months pregnant and her belly was large and she lay on the bed, naked, and wouldn't look at me.

"I'm ugly," she said.

"You're beautiful," I said, playing with her long blonde hair.

She turned to me and said, "You're very weird."

Maybe I was weird. I put my head on her stomach and felt her baby kick. I heard sounds in there. "Life," I said, because I didn't know what the word meant. "The garden and the fruit."

I didn't know who Helen was. She didn't want me to know. I didn't know where she lived with her husband. I began to think she was making the husband up, that the ring on her finger meant nothing, but she showed me pictures of her with him. He was tall and had a beard, a nice smile. He looked like a nice guy and I said so.

"He's not all that nice," Helen said. "Sometimes he can be an asshole."

"Oh?"

"He's hit me," she said, "and he says mean things sometimes."

"Why don't you leave him?"

She said, "I love him."

"That's love?" I asked.

She said, "Yes."

She touched my face with her hand and gently slapped me.

I said, "You could leave him and have the baby on your own, or with me. I'll be with you; I always want to be with you."

"Don't say things like that," she told me, taking her hand from my face. She said, "He's my husband, I'm married, I love him, I won't leave him."

"But you're here," I said.

"I'm here," she said, "but you're certainly not the first man I've had an affair with."

***

She was taking a class at the university, a night class, for graduate credit, the same one I was in. I had noticed her in the class, long legs, all that hair, her clothes, which were businesslike but sexy: snappy skirts with high slits, and open-toed pumps that revealed small toenails colored with opaque polish. We talked one day while waiting outside the office of the professor of this class. I walked her to her car later, asked her if she wanted a drink.

"I'm married," she'd said, showing me the ring.

"Oh."

"But I'll have a soda with you," she'd said.

She stopped coming to see me some time in her seventh month. I didn't hear from her except for a single message on my answering machine: I haven't forgotten about you, but right now isn't a good time.

I found another lover. There are always other lovers, but never the one you really want. I wanted Helen. I had dreams of Helen. I dreamt that we were sleeping in the same bed, that we actually had the chance to spend the night together and that we had made love, but I woke up late and she was gone, she had gone early, had left the bed without waking me, like an army secretly moving from its post in the night without the enemy's regard. In the dream she left a package, a wrapped package, a present; I opened it and inside were baby clothes for a little girl.

I tried to think what her life was, where it was, somewhere in this city, and I ached. I didn't like how I felt, but I guess you're not supposed to.

"Can I slap you?" I asked my new lover.

"If you want," she said.

I slapped her when we made love, but gently. I wanted to hurt her like Helen's husband hurt Helen. I couldn't. I wanted the soft things.

Months later Helen called and said she wanted to see me. "Come over," I said. "I'm still at the same place." "I can't come there," she said. "I don't want to." She asked if I'd meet her at the park.

When I saw her, I embraced her, kissed her as if one of us had been on a tour of duty and now returned. She was distant, as if she didn't want me to be close. I couldn't blame her. She looked good, in a long skirt and blazer; thin now, with no baby in her stomach.

The baby, a boy, was in a carriage, asleep. I sat down with the mother and her child on a park bench.

"I'm sorry I didn't keep in touch," she said.

"It's okay."

"Things," she said.

"I know," I said.

She asked how I'd been and I gave her a smile. I couldn't help myself, I reached to kiss her, but I kissed her cheek, and ran my tongue to her neck, then moved away.

"That's nice," she said. "I like that."

I asked how things were going with her husband.

"Same as always," she said, "but now we're parents."

"Does he still hit you?" I asked.

"Not as much," she said, "but sometimes I wish he would."

"Why?"

"I like it," she told me, looking at me with her blue eyes. "I like it because I like to feel alive."

"We're alive," I said, looking at the carriage.

"Sometimes I don't feel like it," she said. "That's why I have affairs. But it's not so easy now because I have this baby to look after. You were the only one who liked me when I was pregnant, so I didn't think you'd mind."

I took her hand and said I still wanted her and would always want her.

She looked at the sky and said, "Oh my, oh."

I peered in on her baby boy and asked, "Does he resemble his father?"

She said, "No."

She added, "I've been wondering if this is really my husband's kid."

I looked at her.

She said, "It could be one of several others. I told you that you weren't the only affair. I'm not so sure who—"

I asked, "How many?"

She said, "Does it matter?"

I leaned back on the bench.

She said, "Now you don't want me."

"Maybe the baby is mine," I said.

"Impossible," she said. "We didn't know each other until—"

"It should be mine," I said.

"He, he's a he."

"He should be mine," I said. "I would like that."

"I'd like that, too," she said.

We listened to kids playing in the park, cars driving by.

She said, "Four."

I said, "What?"

She said, "I had brief affairs with four other men around the same time, so any of them could be the father, but maybe he's my husband's baby after all. I don't know."

I said, "Helen."

I moved close to her.

"Take me home with you," she said.

"With the baby?"

"Do you mind?"

"No," I said.

"I can only stay awhile," she said.

I held her. There were tears on my chest.

"I'm not bad," she murmured. I just can't help my-self. I find men attractive and I like sex so much and I can't help the things I feel, the things I do."

I told her it was okay.

"The fruit," she whispered, "the tree—"

"What?" I said.

"The garden," she said.

You Will Not Believe What Happens to Me, But Does it Matter? It Only Matters That I Know What Happens

1.

The night my daughter is born, I spend it with a hooker and her deranged ex-boyfriend.

2.

In the delivery room: I see it happen, I see my daughter come out of my wife and it is the most beautiful, smelly, disgusting, strange, wonderful, perverse thing I have ever been witness to. I'm not sure what smells or looks queerer: my purple bloody infant or the afterbirth that follows, which seems like something out of a science-fiction movie.

My wife sleeps. I pace. Don't know what to do.

Look in on my baby girl in the newborn nursery. Don't know what to do. She looks like a stranger to me.

3.

Go out for a drive. My body: it shakes. Have no friends.

We have just moved into this town where I have a new job at the university as a lecturer in 19th century British literature. So I have no one to celebrate with. A new father should be passing out cigars, having drinks with his guy friends. Feel like something is missing in my life.

I drive past a stripper bar.

4.

You will not believe what happens to me, but does it matter? It only matters that I know what happens.

5.

Arrive at 11 P.M. A slow night. There are more dancers than customers—ten of them, six of us. Men come and go and I know this is a business that operates in waves.

A young woman with dark hair and brown skin, early 20s, immediately sits next to me. She asks if I would be kind enough to buy her a drink. I say sure. She says, "Can I have a double?" Why not. It costs $10. My beer: $5.

"You're good looking," she says.

"Thanks. You tell that to all the guys."

"I mean it. Honestly, we don't get many good-looking men in here. Take a look."

I look at all the other men—one in a wheelchair, the others in their 50s-60s, one in a plumber's shirt, all overweight. Two of them, however, sit in a booth with five dancers. They are all drinking.

"You look like trouble," my dancer says.

"I'm not."

"I mean, like you could get me into trouble."

"I won't."

"My name is Angelfood. Would you like a couch dance?"

"Not yet."

She says couch dances range $20-40 per song, depending on the "quality" of the dance.

"The sign out front says 'do not touch the dancers.'"

She grabs my hand and puts it on her left breast. "Yeah, well, that doesn't mean we can't touch you."

Physically, I am not attracted to Angelfood; she is too top heavy for my personal preference, but I do like her youth and innocence, faked or real. I buy a couch dance from her. She asks for the $20 upfront. She is indeed new; she is not very good at this act or not as good as I am used to, as I expect. Here is a case where I apply symbolic interaction to a couch dance: the meaning it has for me, how I interpret her dancing and react to it. Angelfood goes through three positions of dancing: in my lap, her back facing me; straddling me, allowing my face between her breasts; standing up, her back to me, her rear end close to my face. She goes through these motions several times, mechanically, and I do not respond in a positive way. When the song is over, she asks if I want another I shake my head. She asks for a tip. I give her $5. She asks if she can sit with me, if I would buy her another drink. "I won't be offended if you say no or want to sit with someone else," she says. I tell her I want to mingle.

Avoid other dancers sitting by moving from table to table, watching the stage show. There are always two women on at the same time, each at either end of the stage, by the pole.

A large group of young women, all blonde, walk

in. They are from a bachelorette party, or a sorority. They are slumming. They look at the dancers and turn up their noses.

A dancer on stage interests me. She has the body type I'm attracted to; her hair wildly sticks out, and she looks angry. Go to the edge of the stage and hold out three $1 bills. She allows me to place them in the front of her g-string, allows me to touch what little pubic hair she has. She presses her breasts into my face and goes, "Oops." She grabs one of my hands and puts it on her rear end. "How about a dance later?" she says.

She joins me. Buy her a double drink—vodka and Red Bull. Says her name is Brianna, "but my real name is Cheryl," she lies. I know how dancers use the "this is my real name" tactic as manufactured intimacy, to make a customer "feel" as if he is getting something special, a sneak peak into her secret life. I don't tell her I know all the tricks because I have dated exotic dancers, lived with one for nine months and another for three.

She says she is a single mother, has two sons—one is seven months, the other is three years old. "My little men," she says proudly.

"You look pretty good for having given birth seven months ago," I say.

She seems to blush. "Thanks. I work out."

Both her children have different fathers. She is twenty-three. Like Anglefood, she wants to go to college in the near future. "This is a college town," I say.

"I'll go to IVT first," she says, which is Indiana Valley Tech, "then transfer to IU or Purdue—or as I call it, Purdon't."

I gesture to the group of sorority girls. "What's their story?"

She shrugs. "Who knows, who cares. College bitches, lesbians, anthropologists."

"Really?"

"We get people who come in here and study us from the school."

The father of her youngest is in jail. "I hope he stays there," she says, "he's bad news. He was on meth. Always stole money from me. He wanted to knock me up to keep me, so I could make money for him here. Then he got busted. It's for the best."

I don't ask her why she stayed with a man who took her money.

Brianna yells at the group of blonde girls, "Hey, why don't some of you cuties get up and show us what you got. C'mon, get on stage."

"Gross," one of them says.

They just stare at Brianna like they can't believe she's real.

"Cunts," she says, and to me: "Let's go to the couches. I promise you it will be good, better than you expect. I want to give these bitches a real show."

Her couch dance is a world of difference than Angelfood's. Brianna lets me touch her anywhere I want, lets me fondle and caress her small breasts. She kisses me on the lips. She puts her hand between her legs and tells me to rub. She stands on the couch and puts my face into her crotch. She gets on her knees, touches me between the legs. "No underwear!" she says.

"Not tonight."

"Going commando," she says. She has my penis in her hand; my khaki pants the only thing between our flesh. She puts it in her mouth, licking my pants. I have never had a dancer in the states do this; dancers in Tijuana do it all the time, but they all double as prostitutes as well.

Another dancer sees Brianna do this and says, "Oh, you naughty thing!"

"Hey," says Brianna, "at least I don't take it out and suck it like some do."

"Guilty!"

"Really?" I say.

"You can get a blowjob if you want," she says quietly, and then in my ear: "Not here, but in the back, if you want."

6.

Her car is in back; a small, beat-up car. We sit in it. I hand Brianna two $20 bills.

7.

You have to understand something—my wife used to give me great blowjobs when we were dating but has not put my penis in her mouth in four years. I forgot how wonderful blowjobs are until Brianna put my penis in her mouth and I realized what I had been missing these past four years.

8.

Stay in the club and watch Brianna and the other women until it is closing time. Take some money out of the convenient on-site ATM machine. Brianna gives me two more couch dances. She asks what I am doing for the rest of the night—or morning.

"Nothing."

"Wanna come to my place and…"

I ask how much.

"$200 an hour," she says.

9.

Follow Brianna's car to her apartment, three miles away. She takes my hand as we go inside.

10.

Her boyfriend is waiting inside. He smokes crack from a crack pipe.

"It's about time," he says.

"What are you doing," she says, "you're not supposed to be here."

"I'm home," he says.

"This is not your home," she says.

Start to back away. I want out.

"Who is this?" he says, looking at me, exhaling crack.

"No one," she says; "a friend."

"A friendly friend," he says; "more like a trick. A trick."

"None of your," she starts to say.

"You like fucking whores?" he asks me.

She screams. She jumps toward him and attacks him. She scratches his face. He punches her in the stomach. There is blood.

Start to leave and then they both attack me and hold me down on the floor. The boyfriend is on my back.

"Where do you think you're going, John?" the boyfriend says to me.

Brianna smokes some crack. "Trick," she says, "trick with a little dick."

"She's spoiled," the boyfriend goes, "I'm a thick 11 inches."

11.

They take all the money from my wallet, demand the PIN for my ATM. At first I am not going to give them that, until the boyfriend holds a knife to my neck. Give him the wrong PIN. Fuck these two.

12.

There is something else I have to endure with a knife to my neck. The boyfriend goes, "So you came here to get laid, I don't want you to leave unlaid and unhappy," and pulls my pants down and sodomizes me.

Brianna cheers him on as he does this, smoking crack; she sits there smoking and watches her boyfriend fuck me in the ass.

13.

They take my car keys, say I have to walk. Walk funny; a man raped me with an 11-inch penis, anyone would walk funny.

Stumbled into the street and get hit by an oncoming truck.

The next thing I know, I'm in the hospital ICU, the same hospital where my wife and new daughter are on another floor.

14.

Everything I just told you is a lie. None of it happened. It's a fantasy I have when I drive by the stripper bar. When I take a U-turn to go to that bar, I slam into a speeding truck. It's a bad accident. The next thing I know, I am in the hospital ICU, the same hospital where my wife and new daughter are on another floor.

15.

That story is also a lie. It sounds good, though. Both stories have a moral base—you're a family man, you have no business in a stripper bar, only bad things will happen to men who cheat.

16.

I'm not sure this newborn baby girl is mine. I look at her from the other side of the glass partition and she does not look like me. I have thought for some time that my wife was cheating, with more than one man, maybe with a friend. This is some other man's child.

17.

"I'm so happy," my wife says as she breastfeeds the little baby girl in the hospital room. "Aren't you happy?" she says. "You're a Daddy now," she says.

I smile and think about leaving the hospital and going somewhere—a stripper bar, maybe.

It's Very Cold Down Here

"What do you mean what you said about what you said!" said twenty-seven-year-old Ripped van Wrinkle when he abruptly and unexpectedly woke up from a forty-five day coma and found himself inside a science station at the South Pole.

A man with a long thick beard said: "Hey, doc, surfer guy is awake."

Ripped asked: "Who are you?"

The man with a long thick beard said: "The real question is, who are *you?*"

Ripped noticed, then, he was lying on a flat metal bed in what seemed like a doctor's office. He was wearing what seemed like a patient's blue gown; this was not what he was wearing when he was out in the New Zealand ocean; he had been in his favorite black body suit, that's what he last recalled.

A short woman in her late 50s with white hair and thick glasses, wearing a white doctor's smock and a stethoscope around her neck, waddled into the room (like a penguin, Ripped thought). "Well," she said, "the Mystery Man is finally awake. I bet you're hungry."

As a matter of fact, his stomach was growling

and hurt.

"...in the hospital?" he asked.

"Not exactly," she said. "Sickbay."

Two other men with long scraggly beards and hair in ponytails entered the area. "Hey," one said, "the dude is awake."

"Doooooooood," said the other, wanting to high five.

Ripped did not want to high-five.

"Okay," Ripped said, "where am I and how did I get here?"

"Oh dear," said the doctor.

"You're in the South Pole," the first man with a scraggly beard said.

"The what?"

"Antarctica, dude."

***

Ripped was alone with Dr. Helen Mann in sickbay. The bearded men had brought him some food—macaroni and cheese and canned peaches. He ate it fast and wanted more. Dr. Mann told him to take it easy.

"Tell me the last thing you recall," she said.

"I was out on the water, catching some waves. I'm a competitive surfer. I live in San Diego, California, in a place called Ocean Beach. I was in Auckland for a big comp. I was, I was practicing, you know, gotta keep it up. I," and he had to think; "I think I fell asleep on my board."

"Indeed you did."

"And I woke up here."

"Oh my."

"What is it, doc?"

"Here's what I know, as best I know," she said. "You fell asleep on your board, as you said, and you drifted all the way to the South Pole."

"How is that possible?"

"You went into some kind of coma."

"I don't understand, coma."

"I don't know how long it took you to drift from Auckland to here, but you've been asleep in sickbay forty-five days now."

"Wow," he said. "I didn't even dream."

"You kept saying 'Rosebud' in your sleep. Is that the name of your surfboard?"

"It's what I call my girlfriend's..."

"Oh."

"Sorry."

"It's okay."

"So you found me out in the water?"

"Not exactly. Half a dozen Emperor penguins carried you here, with your board." She nodded at the surfboard leaning against the wall.

"Emily," he said, smiling fondly, "she and I have been through a lot. Wait, did you say *penguins* carried me?"

"Yes."

"How? They're small."

"Ever seen an Emperor penguin?"

"They're big?" he asked.

"Indeed."

"That's very kind of them," he said, after thinking about it.

"They're full of surprises," Dr. Mann said.

***

The Emperor penguins who had carried him to the science station wondered about him now and then. They had rescued Ripped from the waters because they were afraid killer whales would eat him. Eventually, killer whales ate all six of the penguins that carried Ripped, so his story was forgotten among their tribe.

This calls to mind something Bernard Stonehouse[1] once said: "I have the impression that, to penguins, man is just another penguin—different, but predictable, occasionally violent, but tolerable company when he sits still and minds his own business."

***

"I need to contact my people, my girl," Ripped said. "You have phones here, right? How do you get out of the South Pole? Helicopter? Plane? Boat?"

"Um, that's the problem," the doctor said.

"What?"

"It's winter here. Twenty-four hours of darkness. The conditions are so harsh we can't even leave the station, and no transports. Too dangerous."

"Are you serious?"

"Afraid I am."

"How long we talking?"

"Four months."

---

1. Dr. Bernard Stonehouse first visited Antarctica in 1946 as a Royal Navy pilot for the Falkland Islands Dependencies Survey (later the British Antarctic Survey). He studied penguins and seals on the Antarctic Peninsula, and king penguins on South Georgia. At the Scott Polar Research Institute in Cambridge, Mass., he edited the journal, Polar Record.

"Four?"

"Maybe five. Four and a half. But not six, so don't you worry none."

"Wait," he said. "Are you saying...?"

"Yes," she said. "You're stuck with us, inside here."

***

The phone lines were touch and go, especially to the United States. He tried calling his manager in Malibu and his manager kept saying, "What? What? Who is this? Speak up! Where you calling from? What's the meaning of this? Call back."

The Internet worked. He sent off emails. Ripped wasn't much of a writer, so he kept it brief: **I am still alive and in the South Pole. Long story. Keep a candle burning. It's very cold down here. I'll be back in the Fall.**

It would be summer here when it was fall back home.

He was about to send an email to Jolene Nemolavokis, his girlfriend. He stopped. What would he say? Then he noticed there was an email from her in his Inbox, dated six weeks ago.

> **yo, r:**
> i dunno if yr alive or dead or what or what happened but i cant let it drive me crazy anymore. i have a feeling yr wholed away w/ some beach bunny bimbo on a remote island out there or in the mountains of n.z. so you know what, thats ok. if you get this email i just wanted to write & tell you that i met someone here in la la land & weve become close & eye think im in love & ah might even marry him. he has proposed but eye havnt given him an answer yet. If aye say yes or no it doesn't matter b/c its later city 4 you & me. yr a sweet & hot guy & great in bed & you make me laugh & feel

safe but lets face it yr a surfer & women throw themselves @ you all the time. i have to get on w/me life &
so that is what im gonna do. U take care & eye hope U
R ok & having fun which im sure U R.
　　xxoo,
　　jo-jo nemo
p.s. rosebud will always miss ya!

She was a model in Los Angeles, a half-Greek, half-Rus-
sian six-foot-one beauty he'd met on a photo shoot for
some fashion magazine, he couldn't remember the name
but it was one of those generic 200 page things with slick
pages and Photoshopped pictures of the beautiful people,
made to look more plastic than they really were, includ-
ing him.

　　He wrote back: **Good luck, Captain Nemo. Sweet
dreams, Rosebud.**

***

At first, he was the novelty. Everyone on the station wanted
to chat with Ripped, know all about him, and in turn tell
him about their lives, since having a new audience was
also rare. After a few days, though, people lost interest
and he was just another body stuck inside the geodome.
That was okay with him.

　　The winter personnel consisted of several scien-
tists doing arcane research on the atmosphere, ice, and
rocks—they were called "beakers." The rest were support
personnel: the cook, janitors, and general maintenance. One
doctor. One researcher: a twenty-nine-year-old sociologist/
anthropologist named Kate Drew.

　　"I'm doing a post-doctoral study on how people

relate and interact within intense, enclosed structures," she told Ripped, "and I was hoping, over the course of your stay here, you'll allow me to observe and interview you."

He shrugged. "Do I have a choice? I'm trapped here, you're trapped..."

She smiled. She had a very nice smile, he thought. She was a plain-looking girl with long brown hair pulled back in a tail. He couldn't tell what her body was like because she wore frumpy, baggy sweaters and pants. With some make-up and fashion sense, he decided she could be hot on the outside world. "You do have a choice," Kate said, "because ethics requires I obtain your consent to be a subject of my study, and you can choose to decline...if you so choose."

He shrugged. "Why not. All in the name of science, right?"

"Science," she said distantly; "yes."

***

There was a well-stocked library of videos and books. Ripped spent a lot of time in the library. After watching the 213 available movies three times each, he started reading the books. There were 2,417 books, ranging in fiction, poetry, scientific studies, and memoirs. Ripped had never been much of a reader—he was a surfer, after all: waves before books. Now that he had the time, now that he had nothing better to do, he found the act of reading enjoyable. He learned some things.

***

He started to grow a beard. There was no practical reason

to shave and a beard helped keep the face warm. Now he knew why all the other men had thick beards. He had never had a beard before, always kept at least a three-to-five day stubble because the image consultant his manager had hired told him that was sexy, it looked good, that's what the cameras and women wanted to see in a surf hero.

**

"Cheers and all that," Ripped said.

"Salut," said Kate Drew.

They were drinking tequila shots and she was interviewing him for her project. She turned on her mini-tape recorder. "Third interview with Ripped van Wrinkle, American surf hero, stranded here on Ice Station 33."

"'Stranded' is such a—harsh word," he said.

"Circumstantial guest?"

"I've had time to do a lot of thinking," he said. He poured them both another tequila shot. "I have been thinking about fate," he said, "and how there is an order to the universe."

"You've been reading those books."

"More than the books," he said. "I've been thinking I'm here for a reason, like maybe I'm meant to be here."

She poured another tequila round.

"Interesting," she said. "Have you always had this belief or is this something new?"

"Good question. I'm not sure. I think I always have, but I never thought about it. I never, um, put it into words. Like, ever since I was a kid I knew I would be famous somehow. I didn't know how—actor, politician, surfer. I just knew."

"Interesting," she said. "What religious background did you have?"

"My parents were Zen Buddhists."

"Ah."

"Hippies."

"Of course."

"More?"

He grabbed the tequila bottle.

"Oh," Kate said, "I'm getting drunk."

"Isn't that the point?"

They drank another shot.

"I notice people drink a lot here," he said.

"It helps," she said.

"It's a lonely place."

"No kidding."

"Why?"

"What?"

"Why did you choose this place for your research?" he asked.

She looked uncomfortable. "I'm the one asking the questions," she said. Ripped thought he touched something touchy. "I'm the interrogative one," she said, and she thought that was funny because she let out a small laugh and a small burp "Excuse me," she said.

"What about sex?" he said.

"What?"

"Do people have sex here?"

"Oh, Rip, I thought you'd *never* ask!" she cried and jumped into his arms, curling up like a small child, kissing him all over his face.

"Wow," he said.

She stopped. "Is this okay?"

"Sure," he said.

"Do you want this?"

"Sure," he said.

"I've been wanting this since the day you got here,"
she said.

Then they fucked.

***

They fucked a lot, hours and hours every day because,
like drinking and growing a beard, there wasn't much else
to do. When the others on the station found out, which
they did pretty fast, they were jealous at first, and then
they didn't care.

***

Outside, the night was clear as Siberian grain alcohol and
a trillion stars twinkled in the dark sky like a trillion stars
twinkling in the night sky. The southern lights—the *aurora
australis*—danced across the heavens like a French ballet
company on tour in New Zealand. Inside, our hero had a
birthday but he did not tell anyone this because he did not
want anyone to know, to make a fuss, and he did not care.

***

"What do you mean you did that about what you did
and all that!" said twenty-eight year old Ripped van
Wrinkle as he sat upright in Kate's small bed in her
small quarters, waking her up; she was just as started
as he about the sudden outburst.

"Hey, what's wrong?" she said.

"What?"

He was disoriented.

"Are you okay? Rip-o?"

Took him a moment to get his bearings. "Yeah," he said. "Weird dream I guess."

"Guess so."

"I'm okay. Let's go back to sleep."

They snuggled.

"What was that you said?" she asked. "What did that mean?"

"What?"

"What you said."

"What did I say?"

"You said..."

"It was dream talk," he said.

"The language is in code, only the subconscious can comprehend," she said, to herself really.

"What?" he said.

"Never mind," she said; "give me a kiss, honey."

They snuggled, which lead to making love, and then they went back to sleep.

***

A month later.

Outside, near the station, a helicopter malfunctioned and crash-landed in the snow The pilot smashed his head against the windshield, very hard. His helmet was inferior and he cracked open his skull and broke his neck and died on the scene.

There were three passengers: Henri, Axel, and Paul: French-Canadian documentary filmmakers in their mid-30s. They were scouting scenery for their current project, looking for the perfect setting in the Southern night.

The weather was harsh and the situation frightening. The three men wandered in the ice and the winds.

They thought for sure they were going to die.

Then they came across the geodome . . .

***

"You're lucky," said Dr. Mann; "damn lucky."

"We know, we know," said Henri.

The doctor was examining the three men in sickbay, making sure they didn't have frostbite on any parts of their bodies, any signs of ill health.

"You could have died out there, fast," she said.

"We know, we know," said Axel.

"The hell you doing way out here anyway?" she asked.

"Documentary," said Paul.

"On what? Extreme survival?"

"Penguins," said Henri.

"Penguins? How original."

"Penguins are very commercial, very hot, very *in* right now," said Axel.

"Jump on the bandwagon," the doctor said.

Ripped and Kate walked in.

"I heard we have visitors," said Ripped.

"All the way from Canada," the doctor said.

"I *love* Montreal!" Kate said.

"I love Canadian bacon on my pizza," Ripped said.

The three documentary filmmakers looked at each other, then stared at Ripped.

"What?" Ripped said, feeling on the spot.

"Good God, it *is* you," said Henri.

"Me?"

"*Tu*," said Axel.

"Eh?"

"Ripped van Wrinkle!" said Paul. "The missing world famous surfer!"

"Missing?"

"You *did* vanish off the face of the earth," Kate said.

"And wound up here," Dr. Mann said; "this place is becoming rather popular."

"You were all over the news," Paul said, "months ago."

"The whole world wondered where you were," Axel said.

"Didn't know the world cared," Ripped said.

"Awww, the world wuves you," said Dr. Mann.

Kate took hold of his arm. "The world can get in line."

Ripped felt loved and it was a nice, warm, alien feeling.

The three French-Canadians all looked at each other, and then stared at Ripped.

"Thinking what I'm thinking?" asked Axel.

"Oui," said Henri.

"This is *perfect*," said Paul.

***

"This is destiny," Paul said.

"*Manifest* destiny," Axel said.

"I agree there is some greater meaning, greater plan in the course of events," Henri said; "there can be no other logical or spiritual explanation."

Ripped thought these French-Canadian fellows talked the funny talk, especially with their accents, but they seemed to be all right.

He was sitting with the three men in the cafeteria,

eating lunch and listening to what they called their "pitch."

"Fuck penguins," Henri said.

"Penguins are getting boring, anyway," Axel said.

"And they stink something bad," Paul said.

"I like them," Ripped said; "they saved my life."

"Ah, yes, I *love* that angle!" Paul said.

"It is a wonderful angle," Henri said.

"The perfect angle," Axel said.

The three nodded in agreement.

"That would be the title," Henri said: "*Saved by Penguins.*"

"Or: *It's Very Cold Down Here,*" Paul said.

"*Magnifique!*" cried Axel.

"Um," said Ripped.

"The hell with the penguins, Mr. van Wrinkle," Henri said; "we want to tell your story. It is a story the whole world will want to see."

"What story?"

"Of your disappearance," Paul said.

"How we found you," Henri said.

"How you got here," Axel said.

"And your eventual return to civilization," Henri said.

"It will be like when Hemingway crashed his plane in Africa and was lost, and emerged from the mighty jungle with a bottle of booze in one hand and a bunch of bananas in the other."

"Hemingway," Ripped said. "I know that name! I read one of his books in the library. *A Farewell to Legs.*"

"Arms," said Axel.

"Legs, arms," Ripped said with a shrug; "it's all limbs."

"Of course," said Henri, "as you need your arms

and legs to surf."

"Um, yeah," said Ripped.

The three filmmakers looked at each other, and then they stared at the surfer.

"So what do you say?" they asked.

***

"It's almost like an ethnography of you," Kate said, as they were in her bed. "Your unique story. You should let them do it."

"Um."

"You'll be famous."

"I am famous already," he said; "am I not?"

"I keep forgetting that," she said, thinking about what that meant.

"My story," he said.

"Maybe you shouldn't do it," she said.

"Make up your mind."

"Don't listen to me. It's your life."

"You're part of my life now," he said. "If they make this documentary, you'll be in it too."

"Oh yeah," she said, thinking about what that meant.

"They're here, I'm here, we're here," he said. "What else we gonna do down here?"

"Make a movie," she said.

"Maybe I'll get my own star, near Hollywood and Vine," he said.

***

Outside, light gradually crept into the night sky like a stalker on the Internet with an old modem and a slow connection...

***

"What do you mean by that when you said that about what you meant about that!" said Ripped van Wrinkle when he woke up from another crazy dream.

He caught his breath.

"Hate it when that happens," he said.

He was alone in the bed. Kate was in the bathroom, on the floor, vomiting into the toilet.

"Babe," he said, "you okay?"

"Yeah, yeah," she said, and puked some more.

"What is it? Did you eat something bad?"

"No," she said. "I seem to be pregnant."

"You're what?"

"Knocked up."

"Say what?"

"Of all the women you've had, you never impregnated one?" she asked, and puked.

"No," he said. No, he never had. He either wore a condom or the women were on the Pill or took the Morning After thing.

"Congrats," Kate said; "I broke your cherry."

Ripped smiled. He had always wanted to be a daddy.

***

Summer arrived like the placenta from a once-pregnant female sea lion—slow, big, and wet. The ice began to melt. More people arrived to the South Pole, and some departed.

***

Back in the United States, it was a media circus. Missing surfer Ripped van Wrinkle was back from the dead, and on his arm was a pregnant academic he said was going to be his new wife! Supermodel Jolene Nemolavokis (AKA "Captain Nemo") told the press: "What's the big deal? I showed the press the e-mail he sent me from Antarctica. I told you guys and you didn't listen. Did you think I made it up? You did! You thought I was lying! I am an honest person! I never lie! The hell with you people!"

Jolene was not happy.

Ripped's friends and family were happy, however, especially his manager, who wanted Ripped to get back in shape and get back on the board. "You got a little soft down there in the snow," his manager said, pointing out the twenty-five pounds Ripped had gained around his stomach. "Good eating," Ripped said with a bright smile, "and lots of tequila."

The cable news and entertainment programs ran numerous clips from the documentary footage that Henri, Axel, and Paul had shot. Most were interviews with Ripped, talking about his past, his life, his childhood, on being a celebrity, being in the South Pole, and being in love.

"My coming here was a blessing," Ripped said, "and providence. I found love here. I never knew love. I thought I did, but I realized I never did. And now, here among the penguins, I have my cherished one, and I have my child coming ..."

***

Kate Drew, Ph.D., almost thirty and seven months pregnant, was still getting used to the changes in her life: living with Ripped at his beachfront house in San Diego, dealing with his luminary status, dealing with other women who wanted him, dealing with having a lot of money and no financial worries, dealing with cravings for strange foods and the fetus kicking inside her like a giant butterfly wanting out of a cocoon.

She was home alone the day Jolene Nemolavokis paid a visit.

Kate thought it was Fed-Ex, delivering some books she had ordered from Amazon.com.

At the door stood this very tall, very tanned, very beautiful, very blonde, exotic-looking super model in designer clothes, shoes, and sunglasses.

"May I help you?" Kate asked.

"Is Ripped here?"

"No he's not."

The woman walked past Kate, letting herself in. "Ripped, yo, Ripped, yo, you around, babycakes?"

"*Babycakes,*" Kate said under her breath. She knew who this woman was. Ripped had talked about her, and Kate had seen her on the cover of *Maxim.* "Excuse me, I said he was not here and I did not invite you inside my home."

"Invite me in," said Captain Nemo, rolling her eyes. "Ha. Funny. I used to *live here*, you know. Sorta. I had a key. I still *have* a key. I could have just *come in.*"

"We changed the locks," Kate lied.

"We?"

"Oui."

"*Look* at you, *look* at your belly," said Nemo. "How quaint. How middle America. Ripped van Wrinkle, *breeder.*"

"Can I help you or are you going to insult me and my...?"

Her what? She and Ripped hadn't gotten married or set a date. Ripped said Nemo was going to get married, too, but it didn't work out and she was regretting dumping him, especially since he was back home.

"Okay, he's not here," said Nemo, "where *is* he?"

"He's in L.A., for an interview."

"No *shit*," said Nemo, "I just drove down from L.A. *Perfect.*"

"In fact he should be on now..."

Kate turned on the large-screen plasma TV. Both women sat down in the living room and watched the afternoon talk show that Ripped was a guest on. He looks so handsome, Kate thought, in his tight jeans and white silk shirt...

The talk show host, a well-known former model and actress in her late 50s, handed Ripped a large stuffed penguin when he came onto the set and sat down next to her.

The audience went, "Awwwwwwwwwwwwww."

"You read my brain matter!" he said. "Cool!"

"Does it remind you of the penguins who saved your life?" the host asked, joking.

"I wish I remembered," he said, serious, *very serious,* "I wish I could find them and buy them a warm beer and some tasty fish."

The audience laughed.

"So tell us, Ripped van Wrinkle," said the host, "is it possible for a womanizing hunk like you to settle down, be monogamous, and become a family man?"

"Of course."

Audience applause.

"He was monogo—monog—mono with me!" said Nemo, shaking her fist at the TV.

Kate grinned.

He's mine, she thought, all mine.

"Do tell," said the host.

Ripped van Winkle looked into the camera. "Katey, my love, I know you're watching, and I know you know how I feel about you. And our baby. I was lost out to sea, trapped in the Antarctic of my soul, and through you, I found my true self; I found my way home." He took out a crumpled piece of paper from his pocket. "When I was at Station 33, all those free hours, I read many books. One was the journal of Ernest Shackleton, South Pole explorer renown. He wrote this that I found profound: 'No person who has not spent a period of his life in those *stark and sullen solitudes that sentinel the Pole* will understand fully what trees and flowers, sun-flecked turf, and running streams mean to the soul of man.'"

Audience applause.

"Beautiful," said the host.

"Bravo," said Kate, wiping a tear from her eye.

"Bullshit!" cried Nemo, standing up. *"Look* at you!" she said to Kate. "And look at *me!* It makes no *sense!* I simply do not under*stand!"* she said.

You never will, Kate thought.

"Did you put a curse on him? Did he get brain damage down there? None of this makes a damn lick of sense! The world has gone mad! I have entered the Twilight Zone of my heart!"

Nemo screamed and pulled at her hair. One of the extensions came out. He screamed some more

"Sssshhh," Kate said, wanting to hear her love on the TV.

"Oh *the hell* with this," said Nemo; "you two have fun *playing house!"*

Nemo turned, stomped away in her high heels, and left the house. The tires of her car screeched outside, rubber that was pained and confused.

Ripped van Wrinkle was still looking at the camera, peering into the living and into her being.

"Kate, if you're out there watching..."

She went to the TV and touched it with her hand. "Yes, beloved."

He smiled.

She smiled.

Nothing needed be said after that.

***

Oh yes—and they lived happily ever after, etc.

What Happened?

They are fighting. The couple upstairs: fighting, again, like they often do. They call each other names. They hit the walls. Their little baby cries and cries. Suddenly, things are quiet, too quiet. I read a magazine for an hour. I take a trash bag out and see her—the woman upstairs, mid-20s—sitting on the stairs, her pink t-shirt and arms and hands and face covered in blood. I know it is not her blood.

"What happened?"

"What?" she says.

"Are you okay?"

"What?"

"What happened? Are you okay?"

"What?"

"Can you hear me?"

"Um," she says, "huh?"

"What happened?"

"What?"

"Forget it," I say.

"What?"

"Have a nice day."

"You too," she says.

"What?"

"I said..."

"Forget it," I say.

"What?" she says.

"Yes," I say.

"Okay."

"What?"

"Okay."

"All right."

"Okay," she says.

And that, as they say in the vernacular, was the end of that.

Solid Memories Have the Life-Span of Tulips and Sunflowers

I thought I saw a glowing disk in the sky, driving home. Actually I did, I saw it. I stopped the car and got out and looked at it. Other people also stopped their cars. Then it took off into the sky.

I drove home, a bit numb; not because of the sighting, but the memory it brought back.

My girlfriend, Anne, was home. She didn't look happy. I told her about the disk.

"I met someone," she said.

"I see," I said.

"I could be in love," she said.

"I understand," I said.

"We discussed this before, right? Am I right?" she said. "We discussed this. If either of us ever had an affair with someone else, we'd talk about it. I should've mentioned it sooner, I know. I didn't think it meant anything at first. Now . . . it's becoming something."

"What's his name?" I asked.

"You don't know him. His name is Bill."

"Bill," I said. "A solid name. I said I saw something."

"You're not bothered?"

"Only by my memories," I said. "Sometimes I

wonder how accurate they are."

She had an incredulous look on her face. "I could be leaving you!"

"I know."

"*David,*" she said.

"Yes?"

"If we'd gotten married," she said, and said no more.

***

I'd skipped my ten-year high school reunion. My folks had passed along the information, the invitation; the request for a small bio from me. I wrote back *David Hawthorne is alive and well.*

I couldn't go; I hadn't become everything I'd set out to be. In fact, I'd become nothing. I was unemployed, my acting career was going nowhere: three failed sitcoms, a lot of bad plays, never the roles I really wanted, the roles I knew I could do. I didn't want to see people I once knew; I didn't want to see my former best friend, Mark, or my former girlfriend, Ginny, or the girl I really loved, Helen. If she was still on this planet.

I was trying to remember the senior prom, and what really happened. It hadn't actually come to mind until I saw the UFO; you see, the night of the prom I had seen a UFO—I think—and I think I saw Helen board the ship, telling me her real place was with her people.

Or was this a dream? Prom night, thirteen years ago, and I can only recall patches—the rented tux, Ginny's dress, the limo, the hillside party, the drinking, Helen's green dress, Ginny's pregnant belly.

I've had dreams, over the years, that I was having sex with Helen. I've had dreams that I was reunited with

113

Ginny and we were having sex as well. Sometimes I think about these dreams and wonder if they were *not* dreams, if they were really misplaced moments in my life that I've conveniently discarded.

I went to see Craig, a psychotherapist friend of mine.

***

"Hypnotize you?" Craig said.

"Yeah," I said. "That's what I want you to do."

"I'm not sure it'd be a good idea," he said.

"This is just between you and me. I'm not a patient. I'm your friend."

"That's the problem. You'll go from being my friend to being my patient."

"I have to know," I said.

"If you saw a UFO thirteen years ago?"

"I saw one three nights ago," I said. "I may have seen one thirteen years ago."

"Did you see aliens?" he asked.

"No," I said.

"I have a number of patients who claim to be abductees," Craig said.

"I wasn't *abducted*," I said. "And what do you think about these other patients of yours? Are they crazy?"

"Something is going on," Craig said. "Okay, look. We'll set a time for next week. Until then, I want you to concentrate on your memories. We may not have to use hypnosis. If we do, we do. But for the next week, just think back. Focus on details. Try to map out the night in question, anything and everything you can recall. From the moment you woke up, until the moment the night ended."

***

I tried, and I was afraid. I was alone, trying, and I was afraid. I'd come home and Anne wouldn't be there. Some nights she'd be home, some she wouldn't. She was with that person she talked about. Bill—the solid name. What had I done wrong?—all my life, what had I done wrong? This is why I didn't like to dwell on the past: I always rediscovered my blunders and over-analyzed them.

I was going with Ginny my last two years in high school. I had chased her; she wasn't interested at first, then something happened, then we were boyfriend and girlfriend. I didn't know what I was doing; she didn't know what she was doing. We were making it up as we went along. We were kids. We were in love. (I think we were in love.) Yes, we were in love, as kids like us could be in love; but I wanted more. I didn't know what "more" was. There was something missing. I think she felt it.

We lost our virginity together.

She had a horrible mother, a tyrant of a mother, like one of those wicked witch anti-mothers from children's fantasies; the bad antagonist you must do battle with and overcome. Ginny and I certainly did battle with her. Her mother, who we called The Monster, hated me. She thought I was a bad choice of a boyfriend, and maybe I was; my parents were no one special, I didn't have a job or a car, and my only interest in the future was acting. I wanted to be an actor.

The Monster often hit Ginny in the face. "Hit her back," I suggested once.

"She would murder me," Ginny said.

"Like *kill* you?"

"Once, there was this news item on TV," Ginny

said. "About a woman who stabbed her son to death. The Monster said, 'I bet he drove her to it.'"

Two or three times a week, The Monster would ask questions like: "Did you fuck him yet?" and "Are you pregnant yet?"

Ginny answered in the negative; sex was our secret.

Sex was a secret in high school, as well as fuel for gossip—who's having sex with who, which teachers have had sex with their students, what wild thing happened one drunken night. The first item of gossip I'd heard about Helen was that she was drinking tequila in a car with two boys (this was at the movies) and she performed various oral sexual acts with both of them. When I looked at Helen, I couldn't believe this tale of debauched drunkenness; Helen was quiet and demure, with pale skin and pale blonde hair and gold-rimmed glasses. She dressed in skirt suits and fine dresses, and held herself—when she sat, when she walked—like royalty.

It was halfway through senior year that I was convinced I was in love with Helen. And I didn't even really know her! She sat near me in my Spanish and Political History classes, and sometimes we talked (her soft, bird-like voice). I started to have dreams about her, which translated into daytime fantasies. The worst of it all was that I spent my time, then, with Ginny, when I really wished to be with Helen. And then Ginny got pregnant, and I really wanted to be with Helen; I escaped into my fantasies with Helen.

Perhaps I just wanted to escape.

***

When Ginny told me she knew she was pregnant, I went, "Oh." Oh—oh I don't know. I didn't want to think about it. We didn't talk about it. We went on like it wasn't true. But it was there—her sickness, her body changes. She was six weeks gone. I was hoping it would go away. I thought about Helen a lot more; I created worlds of the future for us. She came to me in my dreams. She said, in my dreams, Helen said, "Open your eyes, David." "They're open," I replied, *they are!*"

***

I didn't want to go to the senior prom, which to me was scenes of horror and destruction in that movie, *Carrie*. You know, Sissy Spacek, the meek telekinetic, thought she was the sad little girl whose dreams had all come true, only to find out it was all a practical joke. So what does she do? She kills everyone. (I had a fantasy of Ginny getting those powers and doing to The Monster what Carrie did to her evil mother.)

Ginny wanted to go to the prom, and my mother wanted us to go. My mother took me to be fitted for a tux rental; I thought I looked rather well in it, standing before the mirror, turning sideways, then spinning forward, my hand out like a gun, the James Bond theme running through my mind, the way impressionable young men dream of being heroes. My mother even rented a dress for Ginny, because The Monster certainly wasn't going to lift a finger for this event. I don't know what my mother was thinking, about Ginny and me. Did she think we were going to get married? What would my mother say if she knew Ginny was pregnant? The whole time I kept thinking these things—especially when she took me to get my finger fitted for a class ring. What would my mother say if she knew she were going to be a grandmother?

Perhaps she would've been happy.

I wasn't happy.

I was scared as all hell.

***

Anne came home.

"Hello," I said.

"Hi," she said. She wouldn't look at me.

"Home tonight?" I asked.

"You want dinner?" she said. "I was thinking of making dinner."

I joined her in the kitchen. She was starting to make spaghetti.

"I want a quiet night," she said. Something was wrong, I could tell by her voice.,

"What?"

"Don't ask me about Bill."

"I won't. I wasn't going to."

"Oh," she said. "How've you been?"

"Did you go to your senior prom?" I asked.

"What?"

"Prom," I said.

"Of course," she said, thinking. "Of course." She stirred the noodles.

"Who'd you go with?"

"Hank," she said.

"Another solid name," I said.

"*Please*," she said.

"Meat sauce tonight?"

"All we have is marinara."

"Did you love Hank?" I asked.

"No, no," she said. "He was a *jock*. Football. Someone to go with. He asked me, I said yes. He was a good lay, too. Now that I think about it. A good hard fuck."

***

"So, wait," Anne said as we ate dinner, "you were with Ginny, but you didn't want to be with Ginny."

"No."

"You wanted this Helen."

"I think so."

"You said you loved Ginny."

"I loved her," I said. "Yes, I loved her very much."

"But you loved Helen."

"No."

"You were afraid," Anne said. "Ginny was knocked up, you couldn't deal with it, so you had eyes on Helen."

"That's what I've been saying."

"Geez," Anne said, drinking red wine.

"It was a shitty thing."

"You were a kid."

"It was still shitty."

"What happened to Ginny?" Anne asked.

"She's married, as far as I know," I said. "Two kids. She became a born again Christian."

"I hate it when that happens. What about Helen?"

"I don't know."

"Wait. Ginny has two kids?"

"Last I heard."

"One isn't yours?"

"No," I said. I realized that for all the time Anne and I had lived together, she didn't know me. I didn't know her. We'd never really talked about our pasts, like this.

"What happened to your kid? She was pregnant."

"Well," I said, "we didn't have it."

***

"Just relax," Craig said.

"I'm relaxed," I said. I was sitting in a deep, plush, comfortable armchair in his office. He stared at me with his abysmal blue eyes.

"Just relax," he said, "and listen to my voice."

I don't know how he did it—I don't want to know—but I went under. It's a funny thing. First you think: I'm not really hypnotized, I'm aware of everything. Then you realize something is different: you have total access to the past, and it's happening right before you. You're going through the motions like you're back there again; you're that age. You can feel it; you can smell it.

"Senior prom, thirteen years ago," Craig said.

"Ginny and I are in the living room of my parents' house," I said. "My mother is excited. She's taking all kinds of pictures. I'm in my James Bond penguin suit and Ginny is in her dress. I keep looking at her stomach, I keep thinking about the life that's growing in there. I'm afraid. How the hell will I tell them? Will they understand? They'll understand, of course; it happens. But I'll have responsibilities. I'm not ready for this. I don't want this."

"Focus on Ginny's face."

"She's glowing. She's smiling."

"What happens next?"

"While no one's looking, my father shakes my hand and says, 'Have fun, kid.' He has slipped a one hundred dollar bill into my hand. I'm surprised. He was against renting the limo. He's been drinking, I see. I want to be drunk. I'll get drunk later on, I know."

"Let's move to the prom itself."

***

A hotel ballroom near the beach. It was a nice feeling, arriving in a limo, when few couples here had a limo. There was food, and Ginny and I had food. There was dancing, and Ginny and I danced. There was a photographer taking photos of all the couples, and Ginny and I stood in the line and we got our photos taken: she sitting in a chair, me standing beside her, one arm around her shoulder, one hand taking her hand.

I saw Helen. She'd come stag, apparently, with several other girls. How could she not have a date? I wondered. She was exquisite in her green dress, black gloves that came to her elbows. She wasn't wearing her glasses, and her blonde hair was bunched up, strands falling over her forehead and eyes. I think Ginny saw me looking at her—she cleared her throat. I forced myself not to look at Helen.

Something felt empty, in me. Something felt wrong. I was in the wrong universe. This wasn't the way things were supposed to happen, I wasn't intended to graduate high school and go straight into fatherhood, maybe even marriage.

I looked at Ginny, and for a brief moment, I felt resentment.

I wanted to say something to her, but tonight was certainly not the night.

I was scared.

Ginny and I danced a slow dance. We returned to our table. I was trying to be sly, my eye seeking out Helen—she danced with a few guys, but mostly remained with her friends.

Mark joined us. Mark was my best friend. He was a tall, overweight guy who was into a lot of the things I was: acting, literature, rock music. We had a good connection. We'd spent many nights driving around in his car, looking for adventures that never came to us.

Mark had also come stag, with a couple of other guys.

Mark tried to get dates, but it never happened.

His tux didn't quite fit him, either.

Mark was full of talk, and he was talking to Ginny, which distracted her enough for me to watch Helen's movements.

What the hell was I doing? This was the senior prom! I was supposed to be having fun . . .

"Mind if I dance with your date?" Mark said to me, that usual hint of sarcasm in his voice.

"Not at all, sir," said I.

So Ginny danced with Mark—it was a funny sight: Ginny was five-two, Mark was six-three.

Helen was looking at me. She had a drink in her hand, and she was looking my way. I didn't know what to do. She waved. I waved back. Then I looked away.

What the hell was I doing? I should've went over there, I should've asked her for a dance. Helen was in two of my classes, right, she sat next to me, right—so Ginny would understand.

Ginny and Mark returned.

"Dance with me?" Ginny said.

"Yes," I said, standing up.

"Me and my big clumsy feet," Mark said.

***

I used the hundred-dollar bill to get a motel room. Ginny and I had gotten a motel room a few times—it was an exciting teenage thing to do. We drove around in the limo until our time was up. "You're the quietest couple I've had in a while," he said, "usually proms are pretty wild."

I tipped him twenty bucks at the motel.

"We *are* quiet," Ginny said when we went into our room.

"We're getting old," I said. "This is scary."

We undressed and got into bed.

"Senior prom," Ginny said. "Do you want to make love?"

My hand was on her slightly protruding belly. "I don't know."

"I'm not in the mood. I will if you want to."

"I'm not in the mood," I said.

"Okay."

"Oh God."

"Oh God is right."

"We're talking like some kind of old married couple," I said.

"We're comfortable," she said, hugging me.

There were knocks at the door.

"Mark?" Ginny said.

"Probably," I said.

I got dressed and let Mark in. Ginny pulled the covers to her chin.

"Old man," Mark said, like he was reading my mind. "I come to whisk you away for an adventure. The both of you."

"No adventures for me," Ginny said. "Sleep is for me."

I looked at Ginny.

"Go ahead," she told me. Her eyes said it was all right.

I did need to get away from this scene.

Mark and I left and got into his car. There was plenty of booze on the floor. I picked up a bottle of Jim Beam and took a good swig.

"You're getting boring," Mark said.

"Fuck you. Where we going?"

"Everyone's headed to Presidio Park."

"And that's where we're off to?"

"You bet," Mark said, revving the engine. "It's the end of our lives tonight! Ha! Hey, you think I might get laid up there?"

***

"Presidio Park is on top of this small mountain," I said under hypnosis. "It's basically the big party hangout— people gather and party until the cops come and tell them to leave. The cops aren't going to come tonight, not on this special night. Even cops have hearts sometimes. So Mark and I are there, drinking, and there's all these kids from school, and from other schools too. There's a lot of loud music. It is here that I saw the UFO."

"You see it now?" Craig asked.

"Not now, no. I see Helen. I'm stunned. She's still in her green dress, and those gloves. She's alone, drinking a beer. I know this is my one and only chance. I can't blow it. I grab a bottle of tequila from Mark's car and tell him I have to meet my destiny. Can you believe that? I actually say that. 'Destiny!' But I'm already drunk. 'Oh fine,' Mark says, 'just leave me all alone.' 'Bitch,' I say to him. 'Double-bitch,' he says to me."

"Tell me about the sky."

"It's a very clear night, a lot of stars out."

"Tell me about Helen."

"God, she's gorgeous. She sees me coming her away, and she smiles. Her teeth are perfect and white."

***

"Hey there," Helen said. "Hello."

I wanted to tell her she was the most perfect woman in the world; I wanted to tell her she was the invader of my dreams.

"Hi," I said.

"Nice tequila bottle," she said.

"Yes," I said. "Yes, it is."

I took a drink. She was just looking at me. "Would you like some?" I said.

"Sure." She tossed her beer away, took the bottle, and took a good long swig.

"So," I said, looking at all the people here.

"Where's Ginny?" she asked.

"Not here."

"Oh."

"She's not—"

"It's okay."

"What?"

We looked at one another. What the hell was going on here?

"I know this *spot*," she said. "Do you want to go?"

Oh, yes I did.

***

"She takes my hand," I said to Craig. "My hand is in her small hand, and we're leaving the general party area. She seems to know where she's going. She knows this place well. I've only been up here a few times. She's been up here many times. She's gotten fucked-up up here, I know, she's drank and smoked pot and maybe even had sex with a few guys. Then she says something to me, which scares me. Like she's reading my mind. She says, 'Yes, I've been up here many times.' We're on the other side of the park, alone, and it's dark, and we can see almost all of the city—at least this part of the city on this side. Helen and I sit under a tree, and we drink from the tequila bottle."

***

"It's nice here," I said to her.

"Put your arm around me," Helen said.

I did.

She leaned into me. "That's nice."

"Yeah," I said.

"I know," she said. "I've seen it in your eyes. I've felt you looking at me."

"What?"

"*I know*," she said, and kissed me.

I was nervous.

"Are you okay?" she asked.

"Yeah," I said.

"I'm being abrupt," she said.

I kissed her. It was a long kiss. She stopped me.

"I know what you want, David," she said.

"You think I'm bad," I said. "Here I am, with you here, and I have a girlfriend—"

"And she's pregnant," Helen said.

"What?"

She smiled. "Come on."

"How'd—how'd you know?"

"Girls know," she laughed. "And I'm psychic."

"Oh," I said.

We were silent, and both took drinks from the bottle.

"I've seen her sick in the bathroom," Helen said. "I've seen her eating crackers. It's so obvious."

"Oh," I said, and drank.

"You're not ready," she said.

"No."

"It sucks."

"It does."

"I like you."

"You should've been my prom date," I said suddenly.

"No," she said. "No. And," she said, "you don't love me."

"I do love you!"

"No."

"You've been in my dreams," I said.

"I know," she said. "Because you keep *thinking* about me. I feel your thoughts. So I go into your dreams."

We drank.

I laughed. "Are you a witch?"

"You're getting drunk."

"You're not?"

"Not yet."

"Get drunk with me."

"I will."

"And?"

"And?"

"And," I said.

"You want to screw me," Helen said. "That's all you *really* want."

***

"And?" Craig said.

I was silent, which prompted him.

"We're kissing," I said. "Man, are we kissing. Her lipstick is all over me, and her perfume. I'm grabbing at her tits and she's rubbing my cock. I try to unzip her dress, from the back. Then something funny happens. Helen pushes me away; she has this weird look on her face. I ask her what's wrong. She says, 'There is much you don't understand.' She doesn't seem drunk anymore. She says, 'Look up at the sky.' I look. And I see it. My God, I see it!"

"The UFO?"

"YES! It's right there, hovering near us. Well—not at first. At first, it's just this glowing dot in the sky, moving strangely. Then it gets bigger, coming toward us. Then it is there. Huge. Disk-shaped. Flying saucer, but really just a lot of glowing light. I look at Helen and she's smiling. 'I have to go,' she says, 'do you want to go with me?'

"The light is intense, too intense. It hurts my eyes. I scream. I'm scared. NO! NO! THIS ISN'T WHAT I WANT!"

I screamed.

"David," Craig said, "you're coming out from the memory on the count of three—one, two, three!" He clapped his hands.

I caught my breath. "Shit."

***

"Shit," Anne said, "you're bullshitting me."

"No," I said, "I remember now."

"So there's this UFO there, and she what?"

"Yeah," I say. "And she tells me, 'I have to go home now.' 'I have to return to my people.' I'm like, 'What?' and Helen goes, 'I was hoping we'd have a moment, but my people are calling me back.' The next thing I know, she's standing under the ship, and this beam of light comes down, engulfing her, and she disappears."

"And?"

"And then I watch the UFO fly away."

"And?"

"I don't know," I said. "I remember walking back to the party. The cops were there, dispersing people. Mark grabbed me and said, 'Let's go!' In the car, he said, 'Where the hell did you take off to?' I said, 'I don't know.' And I really didn't. I was in a daze. Mark thought I was drunk off my ass."

"And Ginny was at the motel room."

"Yes."

***

Ginny wasn't in bed. The bathroom door was closed, and I heard her crying. The door was locked.

"Ginny," I said.

"Go away," she said.

"Let me in," I said.

"No," she said, crying.

"LET ME IN!"

She opened the door. She was a mess. She pointed to the toilet. There was blood everywhere.

"It's gone," she said.

**

Anne and I washed the dinner dishes together.

"She had a miscarriage," Anne said.

"Yeah," I said.

"How'd you feel?"

"I don't know. Remorse, in a way. It was our baby. But also relief. I wasn't going to be a father. I didn't have to tell my parents anything. Responsibility was gone. I was free. I looked into Ginny's eyes and I saw the same, but I also saw a mother who'd lost a child. I think I aged five years in that single moment."

"You were too young. You weren't ready, neither of you. Think of what your life, your life and her life, would be like right now."

"Sometimes I think about it," I said.

"So what happens next in the story?"

"What happens next," I said, my hands covered in soap suds. "We still lived a secret life. We couldn't tell anyone, and I called an ambulance to take her to the hospital. They cleaned her out. Prom night was over. She started to go to church a few weeks later. She said God was telling us something. She became born again. She wanted me to join. I wasn't into Jesus and sin. We broke up, I guess. She met a guy in church, he got her pregnant. They got married. I went to state college."

"Helen?"

"Never saw or talked to her again."

"She went back to her planet," Anne laughed.

"Sure."

"Sorry."

Anne and I went to the bedroom. We undressed, and got into bed.

"Senior prom," Anne said. "I went with a jack whose only interest was to shove himself up my cunt. Do you want to make love?"

My hand was on the wiry pubic hair of her sex. "I don't know."

"I'm not in the mood. I will if you want to."

"I'm not in the mood," I said.

"Okay."

"Oh God," I said and laughed.

"'Oh God' is right."

"We're talking like some kind of old married couple," I said.

"We're comfortable," she said, hugging me.

We made love anyway.

"What about," I started to say.

"What?" she said.

"Nothing."

"Tell me."

"No."

"Tell me."

"Solid Bill," I said.

"There is no Bill no more," she said softly.

***

I drove up to Presidio Park the next night. It was midweek and there were a few high school kids drinking beer and hanging out. I parked my car, and started walking to the place Helen took me to, thirteen years ago. I hadn't been up here since. I had a small bottle of tequila in my jacket. I found the tree Helen and I had sat under, and I sat. The tree looked the same, if memories serve me well. Memory was my nemesis, this I knew. So I drank. I tried to think of Helen's kisses, her skin, the way she smelled, the way her tits felt. I knew those sensations during my hypnosis session, but I couldn't grasp them now. I could only think of the way Ginny felt, tasted, and smelled.

I looked at the city. The sky was mostly clear, a few clouds. Lots of stars, as always. I imagined one star coming alive, and getting bigger, and coming near me. It's a ship.

And Helen gets out.

"Hello, old friend," she says, all dressed up in a silver suit.

I finished the bottle.

None of it ever happened, of course.

I needed to get more in tune with reality.

Walking back to my car, I passed a young couple heading for my tree. I smiled at them. The boy looked away, the girl smiled back—bashfully. I was just some old geek to them, I'm sure.

I got into my car, and drove home.

From the sky, a flying, glowing disk appeared, and hovered for a moment over my car, and flew away.

I got out, and watched it.

I went to the flower store. They were just about to close. I bought a bouquet of tulips and sunflowers. I hate roses. Ginny loved roses. I remember, once, seeing Helen walking to a class, holding a sunflower someone had given her.

Anne was watching TV when I got home. *Star Trek.*

"We're in the wrong universe, David," she said.

"These are yours, please," I said.

She took the flowers, and she kissed me.

The Keepers

Takayuki's parents are studying the manual they brought to the States, trying to make sense of an old tradition fitting for the 21st century.

They don't speak much English and that doesn't help; Takayuki and Akiko's translations are spotty at best. Frank and I do our best to understand.

We nod our heads a lot and Takayuki's parents nod their heads and we all smile like everything is working out well.

Frank and I look at each other and shrug.

Frank is my husband of eleven years, by the way; we got married when we were both twenty-two and things have been up and down but overall a good marriage. We bought a house three years ago in Santa Barbara. Takayuki lived by himself in the house next to us. We became friends. Takayuki works in a biomedical lab and I'm not sure what he does but he seems to make good money.

Frank my husband of eleven years teaches math at the high school and he makes decent money to keep a roof over our heads.

I work part time at a bookstore and make minimum wage but Frank my husband of eleven years doesn't mind. It's supplemental income. My paychecks often pay for airline tickets when we want to travel.

Someday we will go to Japan.

Takayuki had often talked about his greatest love, a girl named Akiko that he left behind in Japan.

One day, Akiko showed up and Takayuki informed us that he was going to marry the woman, finally, and he asked us to be Keepers of the Bride and Groom.

Frank and I said sure, why not, what the hell.

So here we all are, the six of us: me and Frank, Takayuki and Akiko, and Takayuki's parents—I won't even try to pronounce their names—sitting in Takayuki's living room and preparing for a Japanese wedding, or something close to it, that will take place next week in Las Vegas.

***

As Keepers, the job Frank and I are tasked with is to keep the bride and groom on the right and righteous path to the wedding altar. We are to make sure they do not stray or go astray, that things do not go awry or wrong. We are responsible for both of them arriving at the altar in one piece and smiling.

***

I have mixed feelings about the wedding. I don't think it should happen.

"Anne, oh Anne," Frank my husband of eleven years goes, "why, *how* can you think and say such a thing?"

"Look at the way he treats her."

"Treats her how?"

"You know *how*," I say, getting angry that Frank my husband of eleven years is acting dumb; "if there's a bowl of rice ten feet away from him, he won't get up off his sorry ass and get it. He waits for Akiko to serve it to him. When he wants a beer, he tells her to get one and she jumps up and does it. You saw it, that one night, you *saw* how he was."

Frank nods. "Yeah," he says.

"And he doesn't allow her to eat in the same room with him!"

"That's their way, the Japanese way," Frank my husband of eleven years says, "that's their culture."

"Screw that," I go, "this is America, this isn't Japan. They want to do things like that they should go back to Japan."

"You're reading too much into it."

"The hell I am."

"Akiko doesn't mind."

"I think she does."

"How do you know?"

"I can see it in her eyes," I go; "I can see it when she looks at her husband-to-be—sure she knows all about tradition and culture and blah blah blah, but she fucking hates it."

"I hate it when you curse, Anne."

"*Fuck* you," I tell Frank my husband of eleven years.

It's times like these, when he gets me angry, that I want to hurt him with some truth: I want to tell him about the affair I had four years ago with our friend Greg.

For six months, I strayed from the marriage bed and would go see Greg for quick meaningless sex. We never spent the night together. We would hook up for an hour or two in his small messy apartment and then I would go back home.

But I can't tell Frank this.

He's been my husband for eleven years.

I want to keep it that way.

***

Greg had said, "Leave Frank."

"And do what?" I had said.

"Be with me."

"This is wrong."

"Then why did it start?"

"These things happen."

"Why do you keep coming back?"

"Stop asking me these things," I had told him; "don't test me, you know how mad I can get."

He knew my temper, as did Frank.

"You don't love your husband."

"Of course I do."

"Then why are we doing this?"

"It's time for this stop."

"No, no. You can't."

"It's time."

"I love you."

"Find someone else," I had said, "please, find a woman who isn't married, a woman who can love you right."

"I only want you."

"I'm with Frank, we'll always be married."

Greg had said, "How could I ever find another Anne?"

***

I am drinking a bottle of wine with Akiko and ask her what she thinks of old Japanese customs; the way Takayuki treats her now and then.

I am sly about it.

"I hate it," she goes.

"I knew it!"

"I hope it stops," she says.

"Will it?"

"No," she says.

"Tell him."

"I cannot."

"Why?"

"It is wrong."

"How he treats you is wrong."

"Not in Japan," she goes. "Expected."

"The fuck," I say. "This isn't *Japan*, Akiko. This is America. The good ol' U S of A. You can't be a woman of two customs, two countries. You have to choose one or the other. In America, women say, 'Hey, fucker, you can't treat me like that!' Then you kick the asshole in the nuts."

"I cannot," she says. "He would call off marriage."

"Maybe you shouldn't marry him then," I go.

Akiko is shocked.

"I mean, I didn't *mean* that," I tell her.

She goes, "You are my keeper!"

"I didn't mean *that*."

She goes, "How could I ever find another Takayuki?"

***

I snuggle close to Frank that night in bed. I take his

hand in mine while he sleeps. Where would I ever find another Frank?

***

Greg wasn't the only one I strayed with. There was that time on the beach; with a guy I met at a party. Two years ago. Frank was home, sick, and I went to this party of a friend and met this man, I forget his name, and we were both drunk and wandered down to the beach and did it in the sand. We didn't say a word to each other. We shook hands and I never saw him again.

That doesn't count, really.

That's not an affair.

***

I'm pretty sure Frank cheated on me six months into our marriage. I can't prove it and I never asked him. I don't want to know. She was tall and blonde and pretty and was in the same child development class with Frank. I knew she had a crush on him. He was flattered but said it was nothing. Maybe I am imagining it. I don't want to know. It was eleven years ago.

***

We fly to Vegas for the wedding. Why Vegas, I don't know, but that's what Takayuki and Akiko wanted.

There are no other guests.

On the flight to Vegas, Frank my husband of eleven years asks Takayuki about his suit or tux.

"What?" goes Takayuki.

"Your duds to get married in," goes Frank.

"I don't understand," goes Takayuki.

"What do you plan to marry your bride in?" asks Frank.

Takayuki looks at what he's wearing: a Hawaiian shirt and jeans.

"Oh no," I go, "oh, *Frank.*"

"You didn't get a suit, a tux, something?" Frank goes.

Takayuki goes, "Was I supposed to?"

I am this: "Oh, *Frank!*"

"*What?*" he says.

I go, "Frank, how could you mess up like this?"

"Why is it my fault?" he goes.

"You're his keeper!"

"Shit," he goes.

"Problem?" asks Takayuki's father, sitting in the seats across the aisle on the plane.

"No, no," Frank says, "all is well."

"Good," the father goes, "good."

Takayuki smiles at Frank.

"We'll fix this," Frank says; "I'm your damn keeper, we'll fix this. No problem. Vegas has everything you could need."

***

We check into our rooms at the Stardust Hotel and Frank and Takayuki go out, quietly, pretending to hit the slot machines, but really on the search for an emergency wedding tux.

Takayuki's parents take a nap before the wedding, which is seven hours away.

I talk Akiko into going down to the casino floor and doing a little gambling. She's shy; she has never gambled.

"Nothing to it," I say.

First we try out the slot machines, and Akiko wins $200 in quarters on her second pull.

Lights and bells.

"Beginner's luck," I say.

We move to the blackjack table. We have a few free drinks. I'm feeling good and Akiko is glowing with winning and alcohol.

Men notice us. We're both pretty enough. One tries to talk to me. He's in his forties and has salt'n'pepper hair and looks nice enough.

I show him my wedding band.

He shrugs and says he's married too.

"What would your wife think?" I ask.

"We have an understanding," he goes.

I laugh.

I'm tempted. Why not? Why can't I love everyone?

I have to pee and go to the bathroom and seriously consider going to the guy's room for a quickie. It's been so long since I was bad and I'm angry with Frank for not making sure the groom had a tux or suit beforehand. It would serve him right for being a bad keeper.

I return to the table and the guy is gone and so is Akiko. I don't think much of it and play a few hands.

A half an hour later, Akiko is still gone and I get worried.

An hour later, I am in a panic.

I look for her among the slot machines, thinking maybe she's hoping for another lucky pull.

I look for her among the roulette wheels.

I look in the bar.

My heart beats fast.

I'm sweating and feeling dizzy.

***

In the room, Takayuki is trying on a blue and white tux. Frank helps him with the cummerbund and bow tie. He looks dashing enough that I almost forgive him for his arcane ways.

"Is Akiko around?" I ask.

"She's supposed to be with you," Frank says.

I pull Frank aside and whisper, "I lost her."

"What is that supposed to mean?"

"Just what I said."

"What?"

I tell him about it.

"Anne," he goes, "what did you do?"

"I didn't do anything!"

"Something wrong?" Takayuki asks.

"Just that my wife lost your wife," Frank says.

"Lost?"

His parents join us.

"Where is Akiko?" they go.

"Where is Akiko?" goes Takayuki.

"What happened to this man's bride?" goes Frank.

I scream: "I don't know!"

The parents are upset, speaking fast in Japanese. They say to me: "You are her *keeper!*"

***

We call hotel security. They are not worried about it. They won't look at the security cameras. "This happens all the time," they say. "After twenty-four hours, then we'll investigate," they say.

The wedding is in four hours.

***

The wedding is in two hours and Akiko walks into the room. She finds her husband-to-be pacing back and forth, cursing in Japanese and English.

His parents sit on the couch looking sullen.

I'm drunk by now. I have been having one cocktail after another, imagining all sorts of things: Akiko's murdered body in the desert; Akiko on a ship, sent to Thailand to be a sex slave.

Takayuki stops pacing and stares at her.

I run to her, hug her. I can smell wine and something else familiar on her.

I go, "Where the fuck were you?!"

She grins and holds up a handful of casino chips.

"$500," she says. "I win again."

That other smell on her body: it's sex.

***

At the chapel, helping Akiko with her dress in the back room, I ask her about it.

She goes, "I had sex with a man."

"Who?"

It doesn't matter.

She goes, "He asked me and I went with him, to his room."

"Why, Akiko? On your wedding day?"

"I had to know," she says.

"Know what?"

"Now I know," she says. "Now I get married," she says.

***

The words are said, "to have and to hold," etc., and I take hold of Frank's hand, my husband for eleven years, and squeeze it.

What Happens When My Wife's Ex-Boyfriend, Back From Iraq, Pays Us a Visit

J ust when I thought things were getting better, my wife, Anya, talks me into allowing her ex-boyfriend to come by the house for a visit. He wants to say hi, she says; he's curious about the baby and things, she says.

I don't want to put her in a bad mood. The pregnancy was hard; she has, or had, post-partum depression and is on mood pills. She seems to think this is important. The guy *is* a disabled veteran. He lost both legs in Iraq. He was in a truck that drove over one of those roadside bombs. IEDs they call them—Improvised Explosive Devices. You hear about them on the news all the time. When the news of her ex-boyfriend got to her ears, Anya said she wanted to get married and have a baby. So that's what we did.

The soldier's name is Pete. He comes by the house the next evening. He drives a specially-made minivan that he operates completely with his hands, levers for the accelerator and brake.

At least he still has his arms and hands and fingers, Anya says.

We watch him from the window. He crawls into the back of the van, the side door opens, a ramp comes down, and there he is, in a motorized wheelchair. I know the

government didn't pay for all that neat stuff, his grand-
parents did.

Anya opens the door.

Pete, she says.

Anya, he says.

It is awkward. She reaches down to hug him. He
kisses her on the cheek. He tries to kiss her on the lips but
all she offers is a cheek. I don't mind.

Hello, I say

Hello, he says.

We shake hands.

Oh, come in, Anya says, come in.

Thank you, he says, the wheel of his chair almost
running over my toe as he passes by me. I don't mind. I
don't think much of it, to tell the truth.

So where is the baby? Pete asks my wife. Where is
this little bundle of joy?

Asleep, I say.

Nap time, Anya says. Babies nap a lot.

Can I look at him?

Um, he's upstairs, Anya says.

Pete nods. He taps one of the wheels of his chair.
Can't quite walk upstairs, now, that's the ugly truth, eh,
he says.

You look good, she says.

For a crippled guy? he goes. Thanks.

I mean, she says.

I know what you mean, he says. You look even better. Marriage and motherhood agree with you. Always
knew it would. A boy, he says distantly, a son—how lucky
you are, how lucky you are.

I ask, Can we offer you something to drink?

Water, soda, orange juice, Anya says.

Beer?

We have beer.

A cold beer would be nice, he says.

She looks at me. I nod.

Three beers, coming right up! she says.

A few minutes later the three of us are sitting in the living room, drinking beers and talking.

So, he says.

So, I say.

So here we are, Anya says.

Here we are, Pete says. Did you ever think...I mean, here we are, you're married, you're a Mom, and I'm a man without any legs.

Pete, she says.

Think about it, he says.

It's not something I want to think about, she says.

So, I say, to change the subject, that's quite a vehicle you have out there, Pete.

He gives me this look. You know the look. He finishes his beer. Yes it is, he says; yes, it's pretty nice, I'm lucky to have it.

I get up to get us more beer. I listen to them, my wife and her ex-boyfriend. They are not talking. I return with three beers. There is tension in the air. They are looking at each other. Now, I do mind this. The man is in my home and he seems intent on causing trouble.

Thanks, he says when I hand him a new beer.

I've barely had any of this, Anya says about her beer.

I'll take it, Pete says. He quickly sucks down the beer I gave him. Anya and I just watch. She looks at me. Her eyes say don't, don't cause any waves, let's just get through this. I wonder if she regrets inviting him over. He's done with his beer. She hands him her second bottle.

I'll savor this one, he says.

You always could put them drinks back, she says.

And I can handle my booze, he says, saying to me: Don't you worry, none, guy, I can *handle* my beer.

He can, Anya says.

You used to, Pete says to her, I remember right. *You used to put back the beers too.*

Wine coolers were my thing, she says, smiling, remembering.

You used to match me one-for-one, he says, nodding, remembering.

Those were the days, she says.

The days, he says, looking where he used to have legs.

Those days are long ago, she says; I don't drink like that anymore. I can't. I'm older. We're all older.

Wasn't *that* long ago, he says.

Long enough, she says.

Not long enough, he says.

I know they are talking in code, about something else.

Upstairs, the baby cries.

He's awake, Anya says.

Those pipes! Pete says. Maybe he will be an opera singer.

Nah, rock band, Anya says. She stands up and goes to the stairs, goes up and tends to the baby.

Pete and I sit there.

So, he says.

I don't know what to say to him so I say: It must have been very hot in Iraq.

Hot, yeah, hot, he says, and a lot of other things, it was a lot of other things, things you can't imagine, things people like you have no idea about.

People like me, I say.

Citizens, he says, safe and comfortable in your civilian homes. Safe and free because of what we do. We...

He doesn't get to rant. Anya returns with our son, holding him close.

Well looky here! Pete says.

I do not want him to hold my child. If he asks, I will protest; if he suggests it, I will deny it; if Anya starts to hand the baby to him, I will say no.

She sits down.

He's hungry, she says.

You can go ahead and breastfeed him, Pete says. Hey, I'm kidding.

Funny, she says.

I'm kidding, he says. Can I see him...?

She leans forward.

He has your eyes, he says.

I think so, she says.

And your nose, he says to me.

Excuse me, Anya says, standing up and going to the kitchen. I am grateful that she will breastfeed the baby in there.

You're a lucky man, Pete says to me.

Thanks, I say.

No, really, he says: you don't know how goddamn lucky you are.

***

He stays for dinner and gets drunk. We order pizza and he eats pizza and drinks more beer and asks if we have anything hard to drink. I lie and say no but Anya says, I think we have some tequila. I give her a look. Pete says tequila would be good.

Anya gets the bottle. We all have a shot of tequila.

That's *enough* for me, Anya says; one shot is one shot too many for me.

She coughs.

Awww, Pete says, drunk, I remember the days you could put half a bottle away and still drive home—*drive me home*.

Those are days long gone, I say.

Drive home together, Pete mumbles.

He exaggerates, Anya says to me, I never drank like that.

I know, but *still*, I'm wondering about my wife before I knew her.

I can drive! he suddenly shouts.

Anya goes, Ssshhhh, the baby.

Tell the little sucker to wake up and party! he yells.

Okay, look, I say.

I CAN DRIVE! he screams. I'LL SHOW YOU!

He tries to get up, out of his chair, thinking he has legs. He falls right down on his face. There is a *crack* sound when he hits the floor.

Oh, Jesus, Pete, Anya says.

Oh, he says, oh god

My wife says to me: Don't just stand there, help him!

I don't want to touch him; I don't want to be near him; I want him the hell out of my home and away from my family.

Help him, she says.

I help Pete back into his chair.

I'm okay, he says.

You're not, Anya says.

I better go, he says.

No, Anya says. You can sleep here on the couch; sleep it off.

I look at her.

I gotta go, he says, weeping now.

You're too drunk to drive, she says.

I look at her.

He's too drunk to drive, she says to me; he can sleep on the couch.

I know I can't argue with her.

Okay, I can sleep it off a bit, he says, and then I'll go, I won't bug you anymore. I'm sorry, I'm so sorry...

Anya gets some blankets and a pillow.

***

I'm not a happy camper. I let her know this when we go upstairs to our bedroom.

So what are we supposed to do, she says, let him drive, she says.

Why not, I say.

He could get in an accident, she says.

I want to say so what.

We could be liable, she says.

No we wouldn't.

We would feel guilty, she says.

No, I go.

I would, she says.

I don't like him here, I say.

I know.

I don't want him here; I don't feel safe, I say.

What is he going to do? she says. He can't walk. He can't do anything. He's a sad...sad sorry version of the man he used to be, she goes.

The man you used to love.

She looks away.

Love, I say.

I don't know what it was, she says; that was a long time ago.

Different days, I say.

Yes, she says.

I don't like this, I say.

He'll sleep it off, she goes, and then he'll go and that'll be that, she says.

***

I can't sleep. Who knows what could happen. I tend to the baby when the baby wakes up and cries. I let Anya sleep, except when she has to feed our baby. Maybe I did sleep. Who knows what happens in those strange hours. But I don't sleep much.

***

In the morning, I can hear the TV downstairs and it is loud, too loud—first *Star Trek*, then music, the channel is set to MTV or VH1 and the guitars and drums are loud, the male voices screech and remind me of being a teenager and playing my music loud in my bedroom and I not caring what my parents, siblings, or neighbors thought.

Anya gets the baby and we go downstairs. Pete has the remote. He is still on the couch, propped up, and he has turned on the TV, back to *Star Trek* and Captain Kirk and Mr. Spock.

Morning! he says.

Pete, Anya says, shaking her head.

Turn that down, I say.

He just looks at me.

Please turn that TV down, I say; turn it off, please.

He hits the mute button.

I sure am hungry, he says. Scrambled eggs and bacon would be nice, he says. I bet Anya here is still a hell of a cook, he says. It's a skill you never forgot, like sucking a dick, he says, with a sneer, and he says, You're always good at it.

Anya turns around, holding the baby close.

She is upset and I am too.

That's it, I say, Pete, let's get you in your chair and get you out of here.

Don't touch me, he goes when I move to help him; don't you dare touch me, you bastard, he cries.

Fine, I say, you're an independent man; do it yourself.

I push the wheelchair near him. He shoves it away.

I'm not going anywhere, he says. I'm staying right here and you're going to take care of me, he says to Anya.

You're crazy, she goes.

Crazy, he says. I always was.

You're *not* staying here, I say.

Yes I am, he says.

No, I go, you're not.

Not much you can do, he says; go ahead and beat me up, toss me out, throw me in the gutter. I'm a war hero. The police won't like it. The newspapers and TV news people won't like it. People won't like it. You'll be looked at as—as—as—a monster, treating a war vet, a crippled war vet, like that—I mean, I lost life and limb to pro-tect your right to freedom; because of me, you creep, you now have this nice home with your beautiful wife and wonderful child. *Because of me.* Because if I never joined the Army, I would be married to Anya right now and that baby would be mine. She said if I joined, she wouldn't wait for me, she would dump me. Tell him, Anya, tell him this is true.

I know the story, I say.

You don't know *jack*, he goes.

Pete, I just said that to make it easy, says my wife. I was going to break up with you anyway. I knew you would join the Army no matter what, because of 9/11, so I told you that to make it easier for everyone concerned.

I don't believe you, he says.

It's true, she says.

Liar, he says.

No, she says.

She's a liar, you know, he says to me.

I am close to exploding. He sees this.

You want to hit me, he goes, you want to hurt me.

You're pissing us both off, Anya says.

The baby cries.

You're upsetting my child, she says, you're disrupting my home.

Home home home, he goes; *this* should be *my* home.

Get out, I say.

No, he says. Go ahead and hit me, throw me out, he says.

Anya looks at me, shakes her head.

Pete goes, This should be my home, my wife, my baby; this should be *my* couch, *my* TV, and so this is where I'm going to stay. I'm camping out and you'll have to kill me if you want me gone, he says. Go ahead, he goes. Kill me, he goes. I'm dead anyway, he says.

He turns the mute button off and the loud sound of spaceship battles blare out of the TV speakers.

The baby cries.

Anya runs up the stairs with our child.

***

I'll call the police, I say when we're upstairs and putting the baby back in the crib.

No, she says.

He's nuts, I say.

He's hurt, he's upset, he's in pain, she says.

Don't care, I say.

I don't want any drama, she says.

This is *already* drama, I tell her.

I don't want it to be any worse, she says; the police will make it worse. Just play along. He'll give up and eventually go.

You mean just leave him there, I say.

He'll get hungry, she says; he'll have to go to the bathroom. He'll *go,* she goes.

***

He doesn't. He has the TV on loud still and he calls out for Anya. He says he's hungry; he wants her to make him lunch, dinner.

Says he wants beer.

He screams.

He cries.

I'll get him some food, Anya says.

I grab her arm.

Don't you *dare* feed him, I say.

He's *hungry*, she says.
I realize she still has residual feelings . . .
So what, I say.
We're like prisoners up here, she says.
It was your idea. Let me call the cops, I say.
She groans.
She goes, He'll leave soon.

***

For three days, we are indeed like prisoners upstairs. We sneak down, sneak out, when we are certain he is asleep. We come home, he yells at us —
I NEED FOOD! I NEED BEER! I NEED TO TAKE A SHIT!

***

I'm at the local bar and having a few beers with my friend, Ed.
You won't believe what has happened to my life, I say to Ed.
I give him a run down of the events. His eyes get wider as I tell him more.
You're pulling my leg, says Ed.
Wish I was making this up, I say.
That's just weird, he goes.
It's something, I say.
It's scary, he goes.
It sucks, I say.
And you're here, he goes. Here with me.
I needed to have a drink in peace, I say.
Your wife, your kid, he says.

At her mother's, I tell him; I packed them up this morning and got them out of there.

Good, good, he says.

We drink more beer. We're getting sort of drunk.

The guy may never leave, says Ed.

I thought about that, I say.

He's like a grunt dug in his foxhole, says Ed; he's there, ready for war. He wants war, you know.

He wants his life back, I say; but he's not going to get the old days.

What will you...

Don't know.

You need a gun, he says.

Wish I had one.

I have a gun, he says, a revolver.

Really.

Do you know how...

I've fired guns at the range, with my stepfather, I say.

I live three blocks from here, says Ed.

I know.

We can take a walk. I can let you borrow it, he says.

***

There are two things that give me courage when I go home: the alcohol running through my blood and the Smith and Wesson .38 silver snub-nose in my hand. I know he is still there. His van is still parked in front of the house. The TV is on in the living room. He's there, in the dark, his half-body illuminated by the TV and the images of spaceships shooing laser beams at each other in outer space. There is a box of pizza and an empty twelve-pack of beer on the floor by him.

Hey, he says; there you are. I got to the phone and ordered delivery. I was getting really hungry there. Some pizza left if you want a slice.

I sit down in the chair across from the couch.

No thanks, I say.

He asks where Anya and the baby are. I don't tell him. I ask him what he's watching. Not sure, he says; but there are a lot of actors in make-up that are supposed to be aliens of some sort.

The gun is warm in my hand.

I have no idea what you must think of me but it mustn't be good, he says. Now that I have some food in me I can think straight. I feel just horrible. I have no idea what the hell I'm doing. If you can give me a hand, get me into my chair, I'll be going now.

He sees the gun, I'm sure of it.

Or maybe he doesn't.

I want to kill him right then and there. Instead, I help him into the wheelchair.

You don't know how lucky you are, he says.

I think I do, I say.

I'm very sorry, he says.

I know, I say.

Well, tell Anya I said that—that I'm sorry, and tell her I hope everything is okay, and maybe we can talk later, some day, some day down the line.

Some day, I say.

Finish the pizza, he goes, it's good.

And then he's gone. He makes his way to his vehicle; takes him a few minutes to get his chair and body in. I watch him from the window, holding the pistol, ready for anything. He gets behind the wheel and drives away.

I sit down. I eat a slice of pizza. It's cold but tastes great. I have a beer. I watch some TV. I would have killed him, I know this; I was ready to commit murder. That scares the hell out of me and makes my skin feel itchy. I take a shower. Violence is a funny thing, a weird part of life. I call Anya at her mother's house and tell her she can home now.

Fishpole Pete

In the picture he looked normal, and this surprised me, the way I said it to myself, "He looks normal," and wondering what I meant. He was a teenager in the photo, wearing a sly grin, posing for the high school yearbook. He didn't have a worry etched into his face, not like in the other photos I have seen of my old friend, either holding a burning cigarette or a half-empty forty ounce bottle of King Cobra.

"Every time I open the King," he used to say, "that snake comes out and bites me," which meant several more bottles of the cheap malt liquor; he never knew when to stop, he drank until he passed out.

In the photo, he is not yet a father; both his kids would be born to his teenage wife before he turned twenty. In the photo, he is not worried about rent, bills, food, broken-down cars and the tax man at the door.

Remember well the day he decided to check himself into Rehab for the third time, the last time.

"Three strikes and I'm out," he said.

He knew he had to dry out and get clean or else all the booze and crystal meth would kill him, and he had two kids to think of, kids who were now grown and about to make him a grandfather. Rehab wasn't cheap.

"I have to sell my Gibson," he said, "and the trailer out in the desert, and my car. I have to sell them to get back in."

His Gibson guitar was a vintage 1961 Les Paul and worth at least $10,000. I knew how much he cherished the instrument; a prop when he talked about becoming a rock star. That was before he turned thirty. Now he was forty-two and all those rock'n'roll fantasies were just a lot of drunken banter of far-fetched dreams, the way aging actresses in the Midwest wonder what their lives would be like had they moved out to Los Angeles when they were eighteen instead of getting knocked up by the high school sweetheart.

Something always kills dreams.

The day before he went in, we decided to have one last memorable drunk. We hung out around the trolley station downtown, like we did ten years ago, where we used to drink and drink and wax poetic and talk about all the great things we would do and how one day we'd become famous and have our pictures on the cover of *Time* and *Rolling Stone.*

We had a case of Budweiser and a bottle of Teacher's to celebrate the occasion. We toasted sobriety.

"My gravy days are around the corner," he said.

"Our salad days are gone," I said.

We bought a small piece of rock cocaine wrapped in plastic from a street dealer walking by and smoked that. It was cut with soap, but there was enough crack to get a decent buzz.

Another guy walked by, saw us, walked toward us. He was in his fifties, wore dirty overalls and carried a bucket and a fishing pole.

He said, "Can you spare a beer?"

Before I could say no, my old friend, whose name is Luke by the way, handed the guy a beer.

The guy's name was Fishpole Pete.

That's what he said.

He said, "I'm Fishpole Pete."

"I can see that," Luke said.

"I fish at the peer," he said.

"Catch any trout?" Luke said.

"No trout in the ocean. I did catch a couple fish."

We looked in the bucket: there were two fish, and they smelled like the ocean, they smelled badly of fish.

I'm allergic to seafood so I turned away and backed off.

"Can I have another?" said Fishpole Pete. He had slugged down that first beer in three gulps.

"Sure," and Luke handed him another, and then a third.

Next, Fishpole Pete wanted a taste of Teacher's.

"That's some fine bourbon," said Fishpole Pete. And then he said, "You guys got any money?"

This made me nervous.

Luke said, "Nah," although in his jacket pocket was $23,000, from selling off his possessions. Rehab was going to cost him twenty grand, with three to start life over when he got out.

"Three grand for the beginning of The Good Luke Days," he'd said. "Three K of gravy," he'd said.

Fishpole Pete was not happy with that answer. "No money?"

"We're broke," I said.

"You bought this booze."

"Our last dime," I said.

"We're celebrating," Luke said.

"Celebrating what?" asked Fishpole Pete.

"Sobriety," Luke said.

Fishpole Pete laughed heartily at that.

"You two are funny guys," he said. "I once tried sobriety," he said, "right after I got back from Desert Storm. Didn't last long," he said. "Fuck sobriety," he said.

"You were in the war?" Luke said.

"Rifleman in the Army."

"Wow."

"Fucken George Bush Senior and Kuwait," he said and spat a huge chunk of phlegm onto the ground.

"What was it like?" Luke asked.

I wish he hadn't. Fishpole Pete was waiting for a cue to go into his desert war narrative. He talked fast and there was no stopping him. He became violent, shooting air guns at us, grabbing one of us and shaking us and saying, "You know what it's like to have a mortar blast ten feet from you? To not know if you're being targeted with chemical or bio weapons? Do you know FEAR?"

I had a bad feeing about Fishpole Pete. I wanted to get out of the scene; this was not the play I had been cast in. I gave Luke a look, the "let's bail" look.

Luke shook his head and continued to listen to Fishpole Pete.

Fishpole Pete whipped out a long knife and slashed at the air, telling us about all the Elite Republican Guard soldiers he killed.

"I'm out of here," I said.

Fishpole Pete didn't notice half his audience was leaving his theater. Luke kept nodding his head and asking for more details.

Here is the thing about my old drunken friend: he will befriend anyone, talk to anyone, listen to anyone's story. In the past, this has gotten him into some trouble, as a number of psycho cases have obsessively proclaimed him their bosom pal.

It's easy to fall in love with anyone who will genuinely listen to your life story.

I quickly made my way to the car, three blocks away. Underneath the passenger seat was a .45 revolver. Back then, I thought having such a thing in my car would protect me from the unexpected.

I drove to the trolley station. Fishpole Pete had Luke pinned to the ground, the tip of the knife pressed into Luke's chest.

I didn't know if Fishpole Pete was re-enacting a war scenario or intended to kill my friend. I rolled down the window and yelled, "Yo, Fishpole Pete!"

He looked up and I pointed the .45 at him.

"Leave him alone," I said. "Let him go," I said.

Fishpole Pete had had guns pointed at him before, this I could tell by looking into his big brown eyes. He also knew my gun was real.

"Drop the knife," I said, "and back away."

Fishpole Pete did as I said, his hands up. "I was only joking," he said.

"Get in," I said to Luke, and he did.

We drove away.

Luke laughed. "That was insane!" he said. "Oh, *the irony!* What if he killed me, just when I was to start my new life? What if he killed me and found my money! He woulda said God was smiling down on him, and it was his lucky day for all the hell he went through in the war. Man, you should've *heard* those stories."

"I heard enough," I said, and drove him straight to Rehab, where he checked in.

Before leaving my car, Luke shook my hand and said, "Thanks for saving my life, twice: from Pete, and for driving me here."

He did his time in Rehab, two months, and walked out clean and sober.

Three weeks later, he died of a heart attack.

***

His ex-wife sent me the high school photo in the mail.

"It's the only one I could find," she wrote, "and I thought you'd like to have it."

I placed the picture on my fridge, held by a magnet in the shape of a fish.

Have no idea what kind of fish it is.

Branches

avid's a guy I knew from the bar. We'd get
drunk together once or twice a week. I didn't
know much about him other than he could
drink more than I could and still drive.

He said he needed extra work because he had
two kids.

I worry about them not having enough food, he
said. Isn't that what life is all about, food, he said.

I felt for him. I owned a tree-trimming business. It
was fall so there was plenty of work.

I can do that, he said.

He'd been working with me for a week and he was
doing well. He was a hard worker and didn't complain
about his back or hands like some guys do.

One day on the job his wife and kids showed up.
She was a pretty blonde thing, small with a sad smile.
One kid, a boy, was three years old; the other was an
infant, not over six months.

She showed up with a stroller and a picnic basket.

Hey hey, he said.

They kissed. It looked so tender and loving that I
turned my head. David picked up both his children and
kissed them.

Wife and two kids and not even twenty-two years old. I was forty and didn't have a wife and kids or anything. I felt like something was missing and that made me feel like drinking.

What do I owe this pleasant surprise? David asked.

Thought we'd bring you lunch and some sodas, his wife said.

I am thirsty, he said.

She reached into the picnic basket and handed him a canned Diet Pepsi. He drank it fast and said, Thank you, honey.

Are you hungry, honey? she said.

Yo, David said to me, can I take my lunch now?

You're your own man, I said, go right ahead.

His wife asked me: Would you like some lunch?

Already ate, I lied, but thanks.

I just didn't want to share food with them. I didn't have anything against the wife and kid, they were nice as far as wives and kids go. I felt uncomfortable about the idea.

They were poor and needed their food. I didn't need food.

David and his family sat under the tree he was trimming, branches scattered around them like the remains of a battlefield.

I continued trimming my tree, standing high on the ladder. But I could hear them talking and I couldn't stop myself from not listening.

She had made ham and cheese sandwiches and had BBQ potato chips and ranch dressing to dip the chips in. The three-year-old had his own sandwich and soda and the baby drank from a bottle—I was almost afraid she'd whip out a tit and start breastfeeding the tot. She also had a bottle of wine.

I can't drink, he said, not now, now when I'm working.

Well, I can drink, she said.

It was cheap wine, didn't even have a cork. She poured the wine into a plastic cup, holding her baby.

The three-year-old played with one of the branches. This is nice, he said.

I wanted to do something nice for you, she said, working hard like this, I wanted to show you that me and the kids appreciate it.

What's really going on? he said. Tell me the real reason why you're here, he said. Something is wrong, he said.

Nothing is wrong, she said.

Something is up, he said.

The sky, she said.

Maybe I will have some wine, he said.

She handed him her cup. He looked at me but I acted like I was too busy with my trimming work. I didn't care if he had some wine. I had a flask in my back pocket.

She said, My period's late.

He said, Oh.

She said, Did you hear me?

He said, How late?

She said, A week.

He said, Is that something to worry about?

She said, I'm not sure yet.

He laughed, just a little. He laughed and said, I'll pack my suitcase and get the hell out Dodge. He laughed so she knew he was joking.

She didn't like what he said.

She said, That's not funny.

I'm sorry, honey, he said.

***

After work, David and I went to the bar like we always did. I bought him a couple of vodka tonics because I felt sorry for the guy.

I can't afford another kid, he said. Three kids. One was enough, more than enough, and I have two. I can't afford three.

Just get rid of it, I said.

Abortion? No. We don't believe in that.

Didn't mean to offend, I said.

We're not die hard pro-lifers, he said, we just don't believe in doing that.

You like kids, I said, kids are nice.

You ever change a diaper?

No.

You ever sit up all night with a baby that has the flu, scared to death the baby might die and you'd have to live with that forever?

No, I said.

We had another drink.

I might not come to work Monday, he said, I might really just pack my shit and become a piece of shit, a deadbeat dad on the run. I might bolt from this life and start somewhere new where I have no one to look after but myself.

He was serious.

***

Monday: David showed up for work bright and early. We had a full day of trees to deal with so I was glad.

So you didn't hit the road after all, I said.

She started her period last night, he said.

Pictures of Houses with Water Damage

My son sits next to me in my truck and I'm driving him home and he says, "I don't want to go back."

"I know," I say.

He's playing with a toy truck. The toy truck is silver. My truck is dark blue. My son, he's ten, and his name is David.

David says, "We could drive away to another city."

It's not a bad idea. I'd be arrested for violating the court custody order. "Yeah, well," I say.

He knows. He nods. He says, "I don't like it there anymore."

"It's not that bad."

"No," he says, "but I don't like it there anymore."

"Is it because of Bill?" I ask.

"Bill? There's no more Bill."

"Oh?"

"It's Jeff," my son says.

"Who's Jeff?"

"He comes around a lot now."

I can't keep track of my ex-wife's rotation of boy-friends.

"Does Jeff drink?" I say.

"No," my son says, and goes quiet. We're near the house where my ex-wife lives. It used to be my house. I don't miss it that much.

I park in the driveway. There are two cars there—a Camaro and a Datsun 280-Z. The Z belongs to my ex-wife. Her name is Marilyn.

"Ohhkkeyy," my son says, getting his backpack in order.

"See you in two weeks," I say.

"Yeah."

"Want me to walk you to the door?"

"No, that's okay."

"Call me if there's a problem."

"There are never any problems," he says. He gets out of my truck and goes back to his mother.

***

I feel like getting laid. It's a sudden desire; I'm driving away from the ex-house and my son and I'm thinking that getting laid would be nice. I haven't gone out on a date or been laid in seven months.

So I go to a bar. I have some beers and I'm not quite sure what to do. There are women here, and some of them are alone. Some of them are young, some are my age, and some are a number of years older. The beers taste good. I don't drink like I used to. I used to really drink. That's why Marilyn divorced me and I see David every other week.

I start a conversation with a young woman. She has short blonde hair and her name is Lucy. She works at a supermarket.

"So what do you do?" she asks.

"I take pictures," I say.

"You're a photographer?" she says, interested.

"Well, I take pictures of houses with water damage."
She looks at me and goes, "Huh?"

"I'm an estimator for an insurance company," I say.
"Water damage is my specialty. A house gets water damage, I take pictures of it, I make an estimate on how much it'll cost to repair."

"Oh," Lucy says, looking at her drink. "Isn't that kind of boring?"

"Isn't working in a supermarket boring?"

"Yeah, well, what do you expect," she says.

This conversation isn't going too well. I don't think I will be leaving with Lucy to have sex.

One beer later, I'm talking to another woman. She also has blonde hair – it's long and stringy. Her name is Rene and she works at a cyber café monitoring people on Internet-hooked computers.

"How do you like working there?" I ask.

She shrugs and says, "It's pretty boring."

***

I am alone in my bed when I go home. I'm thinking of the houses I have to take pictures of tomorrow. I'm thinking of going over to Marilyn's and confronting this guy Jeff. It's easy to have violent fantasies. I picture myself having a few drinks with this Jeff and liking him when I want to hate him; we become the best of friends and this irritates Marilyn and I'm thinking this might be the route to go.

My phone rings. It's my son.

"I can't sleep," he says.

"What's wrong?"

"Nothing."

"Are you sure?"

"I'm sure," David says. "I just can't sleep. Were you asleep?"

"No."

"Tell me a story," he says.

"A story? What kind of story?"

"A bedtime story," he says.

I've never told him a bedtime story before. My father used to read to me from books when I was his age. I can't remember any of those stories. I could tell him that once upon a time there was a man who led a wild and crazy life, got married, thought he found some peace in having a home and a family, but messed it all up when he went wild and crazy again.

"I don't know any stories," I say. "Why don't you tell me one?"

"That's not my job," he says.

"It is your job now," I say. "I just hired you."

"All my stories are boring."

"Try one on me."

He yawns. I know it's fake. "I'm tired now. I think I'll go to sleep now."

"Okay."

"Good night," my son says.

He hangs up the phone and then I hang up the phone and I close my eyes and it takes a while to fall asleep but I finally do fall asleep. Not even the ringing phone wakes me.

You Can Call and Ask a Question

The phone had been ringing at all hours of the day—morning, noon, night, 4 A.M. At first, the other end would hang up. The Caller ID was blocked but I had a feeling it was she, the one I used to love, and still love; the one that is not here with me and said she loved me too.

Next, the caller didn't hang up but stayed on the phone and was silent.

Speak up, I said.

Nothing.

I could hear background noise—car horns, cars driving by; people giggling; TV shows—mostly game shows and reality shows.

She—the one I once loved and still do—liked to watch reality shows, especially the dating ones.

I started to hear breathing, usually when the calls came before the sun rose and a new day began.

Call all you want, I said.

Silence; breathing.

If you have a question, I said, ask.

Silence; breathing.

Ask, I said.

Breathing; silence.

The answer is yes, I said.

Acknowledgements

Some of these stories originally appeared, sometimes in slightly different form, in the journals *Aux Arc Review, Essays & Fiction, Gargoyle Magazine, Fiction International, Hobart Online, Lamination Colony, Monkeybicycle, New York Tyrant, ONTHEBUS, Toronto Quarterly,* and the anthologies *Prom Night* (DAW Books) and *The Unmade Bed* (Masquerade Books). I would like to thank the editors of these various publications for giving my words some space to exist. Also, I'd like to note that "The Aliens" was adapted into a short film called "Aliens" by Maxim Dashkin Productions.